# When Jess Wainwright's Curiosity was Satisfied

*Wainwright Sisters Book 4*

Andrea Jenelle

Willow Creek Publishing

To every little girl who thought spiders were cool and loved
to watch ants going about their business.
To every little girl who grew up to be a woman who knows
her own mind and isn't afraid to take a stand when she
knows she's in the right.
To every woman who's ever been told it's a man's world
and fought to make a place for herself in it.

# Contents

# Chapter One



The hazy stillness of the brisk autumn afternoon snuck in through the open window. It carried the scent of bonfires and ripe wheat and musty leaves. Jess's students were gone for the day, and she exhaled in relief as she unbuttoned her collar, just a finger length, and lifted the coiled braid at her neck to let the cool air rush over her skin. Many of the farms were bringing in the last of the harvest, and she'd dismissed classes early so the older children could set their hands to the task alongside their parents.

Whenever Jess glimpsed the empty table in the corner of the school room she stiffened. The trays of specimens were still arranged into a tidy stack. The small notebooks she'd purchased for the students to record their observations were still lined up on the bookshelf. But the instrument that would ensure their first journey into the world of science was full of wonder, was missing.

The loss of her microscope six weeks ago had stolen her breath. It had felt like being cast off her moorings - the same feeling that had assailed her when she fell from the hayloft as a girl. The same untethered feeling that had assailed her when Arie had broken the news of their mother's death. Her vision had blurred and her body had morphed into something weightless and desolate.

She'd been morose and nearly inconsolable for the first two weeks - until Davy Greene had shamefully confessed it was in his uncle's study and he'd been the one who helped put it there.

Even as she'd fumed she'd reassured Davy she didn't blame him for the trespass. She didn't tell him what she thought of his uncle - that Cadoc Morgan's wickedness had influenced him.

The man was a relative newcomer to the parish - he'd settled in Heathsted with his two sisters and his niece and nephew three years ago. His origins were murky, and he'd paid cash for the rundown Tudor manor on the outskirts of town. He'd hired an army of tradesmen to bring it back to its former glory, and by all accounts he was fair in his dealings and of a charming countenance.

He was much sought after by the unmarried women of the county. As far as Jess knew, he rebuffed all advances bent on matrimony and indulged instead in liaisons of a much more temporary state. Jess's sister Vin was deliciously enthralled by gossip of his string of dalliances with merry widows.

His penchant for the widows, and the fact they'd never exchanged more than five words at a time, did not explain his larceny.

A fortnight ago, she'd finally found an opportunity to confront him about the theft. That was the first time she politely asked for the return of her most prized possession. When she'd threatened to go to the magistrate, he'd given her an inscrutable look and said he hadn't yet decided what he'd demand in return. He'd then told her he had no intention of keeping it forever.

For the last two weeks she'd been relentlessly badgering him for an explanation. They'd been sparking back and forth like sputtering rushlights, but he hadn't waivered in his resolve. He met every single one of her demands with an enigmatic grin.

When Jess heard boots on the steps beyond the open door, she hastily rebuttoned her collar. It wouldn't do for any of the parents to see her in disarray.

"I'll let you have it back. For a price." The deep voice echoed in the empty schoolroom.

She knew he'd be lounging in the doorway when she turned. With a tousled, uncovered head of rich brown waves the color of coffee and eyes that were the outrageous shade of blue the sky assumed ahead of an impending storm.

She maintained her composure. So he was finally prepared to tell her exactly what the return would cost her. She had a suspicion that if he knew how badly she wanted her English Drum back, his price would morph into something truly astronomical. He was like one of the preening male dragonflies she was cataloging - arrogant in the knowledge of his radiance.

"Is it a price I can afford?" She asked as she worked the eraser over the chalkboard. She was pleased her voice didn't betray the flutter of nerves in her stomach.

"That depends on whether your price is above rubies. How valuable is your virtue, Miss Wainwright?"

Jess prided herself on the fact she didn't have a single tentative, retiring bone in her body when it came to advocating for her students. She'd assumed her position when the village school opened five years ago, and she was proud of how she'd designed the curriculum and convinced skeptical parents and itinerant students that an education beyond basic literacy was important. She was used to confronting gangly boys nearly as tall as she was and emerging victorious. She had a knack for rendering them sheepish and penitent.

Despite her confidence in her abilities, something about Cadoc Morgan made her quake in her half-boots like she was facing down a fire-breathing dragon. He was too everything for her to absorb. Too broad, too tall, too maddening. His eyes too blue, his legs too long, his thighs too muscular. His presence took up all the space and air in a room when he entered it, and she preferred him in small doses, not languidly reclining against the wall like he had all the time in the world to beset her.

She should have known politely asking for the return of her microscope wouldn't be the peaceful exchange she'd hoped for. Of course he'd turned it into a challenge that was an affront to her dignity. She slowly turned to face him.

"I'm certain I didn't hear you correctly. Surely you jest." She wanted to smack the erasers together under his nose and send him into a sneezing fit.

He crossed his arms over his chest and that insufferably alluring mouth curled into a wry grin. "I'm certain you did. And I assure you it was not a jest."

She took a deep breath and brandished the chalk clasped in her hand like a sword. "So I won't be able to retrieve the microscope unless I surrender my virtue in the biblical sense? That is the price I must pay?"

"From what I've observed you are unattached and unspoken for. If you accept my proposition, I will give you memories to last a lifetime."

"The fact I am unattached does not excuse your audacity, sir. You won't entice me to your lair. The ostracism I would suffer if such an arrangement were revealed is too high a risk."

"My lair?" He asked as he raised a brow. He ignored the rest of her protest.

The raised brow seemed supercilious on his part, and Jess was too embarrassed to tell him she'd compared his tall lanky form to a skulking wolf. Her sisters had burst into laughter when she said she expected him to blow down the schoolhouse at any moment. Vin and Gert had laughed so hard, whisky erupted from their noses.

She waved the chalk in a dismissive gesture. "Your house."

The wry grin made another appearance. And this time there was a flash of dimple in his right cheek. It made his face lopsided and far too appealing. "How badly do you want the microscope restored to your classroom, Miss Wainwright?"

His lilting Welsh accent crawled up the base of her spine and she frowned in response. Jess was not going to let him put her out of sorts. "Is that a rhetorical question, Mr. Morgan?"

"No." He was clearly amused by her irritation.

"I'd like to begin a chapter on entomology with the older students in the spring, and the microscope would make the planning and delivery of the lesson much easier." Without the microscope, trying to explain things like carapaces and the way the insect world used antennae would require a hands on approach and observation with the naked eye. It would be far easier for her students to see the intricacy of the hidden world and observe it if squinting wasn't required.

"Then you know what you need to do."

Jess groaned and stamped her foot in frustration. "Why on earth did you take it to begin with?"

His grin disappeared and his gaze turned intense. "You needed to be dislodged from your shelf, Miss Wainwright."

She felt a balloon of righteous indignation expand in her chest. She carefully set the chalk on the desk behind her and braced her hands on her hips. "And you thought stealing my microscope would accomplish that? You thought using your unconscionable theft to press your inappropriate suit was an acceptable course of action?

He stepped closer. "You're flustered. I've never seen you flustered. You're always the unflappable soul of decorum. Like an ice maiden. I've already begun to achieve my ends."

"I'm not flustered. I'm annoyed. There is a pronounced difference." The indignation threatened to choke her. She wasn't an ice maiden. She just didn't believe in wearing her heart on her sleeve or leaving herself vulnerable to attack when she made how she felt visible to those who hadn't earned her trust.

"However you choose to describe it, Miss Wainwright, my act of larceny jolted you from your complacency."

He was absolutely infuriating. Singularly capable of prying beneath her composure like he was peeling away the epidermis that protected her organs. "If your goal was to make me uncomfortable, Mr. Morgan, you may consider it accomplished."

His wink was slow and maddening. "Accomplishing the goals I've set for myself is one of my favorite pastimes."

Jess stepped forward, until the tips of her boots were touching his. "Do you enjoy patronizing me, Mr. Morgan?"

"I shudder to think how you'd respond if I actually patronized you, Miss Wainwright."

"I am not visiting your home to reclaim the microscope you appropriated from my desk." She refused to give him that power. He was already insinuating himself into the design of her curriculum and she would tolerate no further manipulation.

He shrugged. "Then it appears the students will be examining insect anatomy with the naked eye and you'll have to fend for yourself as far as designing the lesson goes."

"You're the superintendent of the school. Isn't denying the students the most robust education available some sort of ethics violation?"

"Not if my beneficence supplied said microscope. And I'm confident my actions are justified."

Jess abandoned the chalk on the desk behind her and crossed her arms. "I refuse to cave to your intimidation tactics."

"May I remind you, Miss Wainwright, that your position here depends on my forbearance?"

He stepped toward her and she stood her ground. "Your forbearance means nothing. Since my tenure here, the attendance rolls have been full. Several of the students have passed the exams for admission to university, and, according to their correspondence with their parents, are settling in well."

"Your position is still secured by my forbearance. One word to the rest of the board and you'll be unable to continue your unorthodox teaching methods."

"I've had no complaints. The results of those methods speak for themselves. And I could simply inform the magistrate that you are holding onto stolen property."

"The methods may speak for themselves, but there are still members of the parish who believe female students shouldn't be exposed to those studies. And you won't speak of the microscope to the magistrate. Because if you do, I might be tempted to tell him about your sister Lavinia and the visits she makes to new mothers under the auspices of her position."

"You're not going to intimidate me into retrieving the microscope. And though we are at odds I believe you are forward-thinking enough to appreciate the options my sister is offering those women."

"It wasn't my intention to intimidate you. I'm simply reminding you that your rebellion is pointless because I hold the winning hand. I'm confident you'll eventually see the truth of the situation."

She turned toward the chalkboard, and reached for the eraser again. She took a deep breath, but that didn't stop her from fuming. "You've made your point, Mr. Morgan. If I decide there's no other way for me to conduct the lessons I've developed, I'll retrieve my microscope. Now, if there's nothing further, I must finish cleaning up."

She ignored the low chuckle and the tromp of his boots as he left.

Once the door had shut, she dropped her forehead to the chalkboard and sighed.

⚬

The fortnight since Cadoc Morgan's illicit proposition had passed quickly. Jess had been occupied with preparations for her sister's journey and the upcoming school pageant.

Cece was finally taking leave of her sisters to chase the origin of the bundle of letters she'd received, and Jess would sorely miss her.

Of all her sisters, she and Cece were the most alike in temperament and motivation and she would be bereft without her companionship and counsel. Cece's departure meant there would be one less pair of hands for pageant rehearsal and costuming as well.

Jess was perched on the edge of the bed while her sister packed a bag they'd pulled from the attic. "You're sure about this?"

"Yes, I'm sure. I need something, Jess. And you do too. What are you going to do about your microscope?"

Jess flopped backward against the pillow and covered her eyes. "Ugh. I have no idea."

"You never truly explained what the bargain was."

"He wants the opportunity to seduce me."

Cece's eyes widened. "That's not what I expected. I thought perhaps it was a kiss he was asking for."

"I might not balk at that," Jess mused. "He has the most beguiling bottom lip I've ever seen. And his dimple drives me mad. But no. Of course a kiss isn't enough to satisfy the overinflated ego of Cadoc Morgan."

"Is there any way you can procure a replacement microscope from the scientific society? Or make do without it?"

"I had to wait months for the society to approve my initial application. Even if I asked for a replacement, I'd not receive it in time for the lessons I have planned in the spring. And I could conduct the lessons without the microscope, but it incites an enthusiasm for natural studies in my students I can't seem to replicate. And I truly need it for my own ends. My paper on dragonflies is nearly complete."

"Perhaps if you told him about the paper he'd relent."

"I can make my case and hope he's sympathetic."

Cece bit her lip. "What if you just went to the magistrate and allowed him to handle it? I'm sure Sir Timms would do whatever is within his power to rectify your dilemma."

"I agree. Things would be far easier if I approached the magistrate. But I can't. He's threatened to expose Lavinia if I do."

"How did he find out she's dispensing contraceptives?" Cece asked in amazement.

"I don't know how he found out, but I know he's not going to forget. He looked pleased as punch when he used it to thwart me."

"He must know accepting his proposal would place you at risk of losing your position. Surely he's not such an unforgivable rogue. Perhaps he's merely testing your fortitude."

"I don't think he's testing me. His stance seemed firm." Jess flopped backward against the pillows again and put her hand to her forehead. "I don't know why he's chosen me as his prey. I've done nothing to encourage his interest!"

Cece sat beside her and patted her hand in sympathy. "If he truly is a rogue, perhaps it's his inability to attract your attention that's behind all this. Like the way Torvin Black used to steal Vin's pencils."

Jess laughed at the memory. "He was absolutely mad for her. But I don't think he's like Torvin. I'm just a challenge because I seem impervious to his charms."

"Have you asked the vicar if you can borrow his microscope?"

"I don't want anyone to know what's happening. As you said, it's a risk. And besides, the vicar's microscope is unavailable. He cracked one of the lenses and is waiting on a replacement from Brussels."

"I wish I could give you better counsel. Especially since you're the reason I finally set aside my widow's weeds. If you hadn't persuaded me to embrace life again and encouraged this sojourn to Scotland that's completely out of character, I'd still be contemplating years of wearing mobcaps in drafty corners."

"I've never been attracted to someone like this. I thought teaching and my studies were enough. But when I'm around him there are all of these things jumbled up inside me, and I don't know what to do with them."

Cece sat beside her on the bed and gave her a contemplative look. "Perhaps he's your catalyst, Jess. Like the letters were mine."

"Why did it happen like *this*?" Jess asked in an anguished tone. "Why does it have to be *him* that makes me doubt everything I thought I knew about myself?"

"I used to ask myself the same thing about Henry. What it was about him that compelled me to accept his proposal and his kiss when I barely knew him. I don't have answers for you, but maybe you should just stop running away from the things he makes you feel."

Jess grimaced. "Easier said than done."

"Why do you think you're so drawn to him?"

"I wish I knew. He comes across as all bluster and charm, but sometimes I catch a glimpse of what he's hiding beneath the surface of all those smiles and his ridiculous teasing and it makes me wonder if there's more to him than that."

"I wish I could be here to offer you advice."

Jess shook her head. "No, I understand now why you're going. You were like me - stuck at a fork in the road with your life shrinking around you. Every day I feel more inclined to accept Mr. Morgan's wager. Even though it goes against my better judgment and all of the ways I've tried to protect myself against people like him. Because a part of me feels stuck too."

"People like him?"

"People like him, especially men, who don't care in the least about the consequences of their actions. Men like him who act as if they own the world and everyone in it. As if the world was created specifically for their delectation - like an oyster laboring years to produce a perfect pearl."

"Can't you treat him the same way?"

"I don't know if I have that kind of fortitude or determination. If I can withstand the obscene pressure of all of that charm and bluster. He takes up all the air in the room until all I can smell and breathe is him and his presence. It should make me feel invisible - but it does just the opposite. It makes me feel seen. In ways no one has ever seen me. In ways I didn't even know I wanted to be seen."

Cece gave her a rueful, commiserating smile. "That's how it felt with Henry as well. And when I found out he wasn't ever coming back, that those letters were all I had, I went back to being invisible."

Jess tangled Cece's fingers in hers. "You've never been invisible."

"Not to my sisters, no. But I became invisible to the rest of the world. Confined to the shadows and a half-life I never imagined myself living. It's why I wore black for so long. Because without the black that defined me, I didn't know who I was. Or how to get back the person I was before Henry or his death."

"Is that what you think I've been doing, living a half-life?" Jess tentatively asked.

"I think that's part of it," Cece gently said. "I think mother's death and father's neglect conditioned us to ex-pect less. To occupy a smaller space and be grateful for the barest morsel of affection. Arie did everything she could to give us stability and love, but there was always something inside me that hungered for more. I think it's the same for you."

"So my attraction to him is some sort of hunger for attention?"

"No. It's a hunger for affection. And recognition. For someone to look at you and decide you are worthy of more. That you deserve that opportunity when it's not an obligation or a responsibility for the other person."

"I don't know if he's the one who can give me those things. Even if I acknowledge to myself I may be seeking them."

"My advice is to give yourself the grace to find out. Take the wager and see where it leads. Don't let him control you or the way things unfold between you."

Jess squeezed her hand. "Thank you, little sister. You are wise beyond your years."

"I wish I could give you better counsel."

"I simply needed someone to confide in. Your counsel has been exactly what I needed to determine my next step," Jess said as she sat up and gave her sister a hug.

# Chapter Two

AFTER CADOC LEFT JESSAMINE Wainwright standing in her schoolroom, brandishing her chalk like a weapon, he gleefully rubbed his hands together. It had taken every ounce of his willpower not to pin her against her desk. The fierce gaze she'd skewered him with hadn't boded well and he knew only a scrap of dignity had restrained her from clobbering him with the erasers.

He might have let her get that close so he could twist her up for his kiss. It would have been worth the layer of chalk dust on his clothes and the tickle in his throat.

Cadoc had been orchestrating everything that was happening for months and Jess Wainwright would soon be caught in the snare he'd been carefully constructing since the day she'd turned his world upside down. She'd addressed the school board, and when asked about the design of her curriculum, the explanation was unforgettable.

It was apparent from her explanation that she was a follower of Wollstonecraft and the Suffrage Movement, things Cadoc supported as well. He'd raised four younger sisters and he wanted them to have a say in their lives. But what had struck Cadoc the most was her discussion of rational thought and how important it was to teach her students how to use it. This was the reason Cadoc had spent his life fighting for workers and organizing the mines. Because rational thought demanded that each individual consider their place in the world and their contribution to it.

After that impassioned speech, whenever he'd visited the schoolroom in the context of observation as a board member, his fascination had become more entrenched. He'd taken note of the loving glances she bestowed on her microscope. It was a fine instrument, and he understood her devotion, but the way her slender fingers brushed over it as she was delivering an explanation, set his blood on fire. He dreamt of those slender, agile fingers drifting over his skin and couldn't breathe.

His first instinct hadn't been to coerce her, but it was the way he'd always achieved his ends. He didn't know how to ask her to come to him of her own accord, and he doubted she would. She was too self-contained, too sure of who she was, to come to him. Unless he left her no choice. That's why he'd stolen her microscope. He knew his mam would be appalled by his manipulation, and that part of him, the one that missed her, was ashamed. But right now, it was only a small part.

He'd instinctively known that pirating the instrument would catch her attention. His nephew Davy had been the one who finally managed to pry the window open and abscond with it while Cad waited in the hedge with his getaway ride. The heist had happened during the last full moon, and it had been exhilarating. He'd felt like a boy again, like the boy he'd never really had the chance to be.

Jess Wainwright's eventual capitulation would be just as exhilarating. He looked forward to unpinning the ruthlessly coiled dark brown hair at her nape and sifting it through his fingers. He looked forward to making her soft hazel gaze cloud with desire.

Cadoc wasn't accustomed to women who intruded on his thoughts like spectres at inopportune moments. He didn't welcome the intrusion - and he was eager to banish it. He was certain the spell she held him under would disappear the moment she was sprawled, thoroughly debauched, beneath him. He knew he should have softened his approach, but he suspected she'd run roughshod over him if he didn't take the lead. And he was accustomed to forcing his will on the world because life was too short and too brutal to sit idly by and let things take their natural course.

He grew weary of the distraction she presented. None of the other women of his acquaintance roused him in any way. Not since he started observing the composed school-teacher. She was like one of the serene swans he'd watched gliding over the lake. Gilded in light and long-necked and graceful. Cadoc blamed it on his knowledge that the harshness of the world was made to beat a man down and break him in half. He'd risen above it, the hard way,  and fought for every inch of his peace.

Jess Wainwright represented that one last bit of serenity that still escaped him.

He had a duty to his family and his countrymen to invest all his energy and acumen in ways that moved the needle of industrial progress forward. Because he'd seen firsthand why the burdens such industry placed on the poor should be abolished. He was determined to do his part. He'd fought alongside his fellow miners for better wages and better working hours. For an end to child labor. Plenty of his bones had been broken for his convictions.

When he was seven years old, Cadoc followed his older brother Griffin into the pit. Griffin had just turned seventeen, and it was Cadoc's responsibility to carry his tools and fill the drams with the coal his brother cut and blasted.

The pit was a hopeless, miserable, scary place and his first day surrounded by inky darkness he never thought he'd see sunshine again. The damp made him sneeze and Griffin told him there were big, hairy spiders hiding in every corner that preyed on toes. Whenever he climbed the ladder at the end of the day, even though it was usually by moonlight, he wanted to kiss the grass beneath his feet.

He dreamt of fishing and running through the meadows chasing after his sisters, and he always thought those things would be his again soon. Until he looked down at the grime on his skin and clothes that no amount of lye could scrub away. Until he looked down and saw the black crescents beneath his nails and squinted into the bright sun he'd begun to believe was forever lost to him.

When he turned ten, he became a drammer. He was outfitted with a leather girth and a chain to haul the full sleds of coal from the head of the shaft to the main road. It was a distance of sixty yards and he trudged home every night with crushed fingers and an aching back. The pickers were ruthless and reveled in tormenting the children who served as drammers. It was a constant fight for dominance and submission, and he learned to defend himself against their blows.  He didn't complain, because the work was keeping his younger sisters fed. He still carried the scars on his back from one of the pickers who'd thrashed him, and three fingers on his left hand had been crushed so many times they'd never completely straighten.

Cadoc was fourteen when Griffin and his mother were killed in a methane explosion. He'd been aboveground, working on the machinery instead of down in the tunnels with them. He was left to raise his five younger sisters, and that's when he knew he needed to make sure no one else died that way - so that those he loved, who had no choice but to work in the mines, lived. He started begging for scraps of metal from the men who ran the equipment, and when he showed the foreman the carbide lamp he'd designed, Rhys Jones took him under his wing. He taught Cadoc how to read blueprints, how to calculate dimensions and rudimentary chemistry.

That's when Cadoc started organizing.

Because he didn't want his sisters to become pit lasses, and he wanted his family's deaths to lead to something better for all of them, he absorbed knowledge like a sponge. He used it to create a better world for everyone who took the lift into the darkness so they could earn a decent living. When their mother died, Gwyn had just turned eleven and was old enough to care for their little sisters, Peggy, Ellen, Caris and Mary, while he became the one who put bread on the table for all of them. For ten years, he put in the long hours to become a foreman and invent things that would make mining easier and safer. He was at the front of every march, and when he started making money hand over fist from his industrial improvements, he became the voice of Griffin and his mother in places they wouldn't have been able to reach.

By the time he turned twenty-seven, he'd invented four lamps to help curtail the methane explosions, a trammel system with rails so children like the one he'd been wouldn't be crushed beneath the wheels of the coal wagons, and devised a way to safely install lighting down in the tunnels.

His inventions had brought a stable, robust income that he'd invested wisely in manufactories and railroads. He and his family would never again have to wonder where the next loaf of bread was coming from. They would never again have to drop down into the darkness and dream about fishing and running through meadows instead.

When Gwyn married a man from Cumbria, that was where he decided to settle. And when Gwyn followed her husband to the goldfields of California, he agreed to become the guardian of his niece and nephew until they were sent for.

Marcella and Davy had been rambling about his manor house with him and his middle sister Caris for five years. Gwyn had borne three more children and she and Simon had moved further north, chasing fortune. Gwyn dashed off a letter every month, but she'd yet to ask Cadoc to send her two eldest children. And the letters themselves had become more and more slapdash and perfunctory. She never asked real questions about the children she'd left behind and Cadoc had no idea if she'd received any replies updating her on their progress. She never referred to his side of the correspondence.

Marcella had just turned seven and Davy was nearly twelve. They'd stopped asking when they were going to America. They'd both become rather avid amateur naturalists, no doubt due to the influence of the beautiful bluestocking they reported to every morning.

In what little spare time he had, he thought about the prim, beguiling school teacher who instructed his niece and nephew.

Jessamine Wainwright was forthright and self-assured and she shared his fascination for science and mechanics. He enjoyed thwarting her so he could watch the color flush her cheeks and throat and spent an inordinate amount of time devising ways to arouse her irritation, so she'd snap and crackle like a fireworks display. There was nothing he wanted more than to glide his hands over her supple curves, and untether the waterfall of dark hair she kept ruthlessly pinned up. Her hazel eyes would flare as she succumbed to his touch and taste.

Just the thought of her surrender made his cock harder than a pike and sent his thoughts into a jumble that destroyed his ability to concentrate on anything else. He needed to send out monthly invoices, but couldn't stop thinking about the way her eyes had sparkled in fury at his offer to ruin her.

A light knock at the door interrupted his preoccupation. "Come in," he called.

His sister Caris walked in, a sealed envelope clutched against her chest. "We've gotten a letter from Gwyn."

He rocked back on the legs of his chair and gestured toward the divan across from him. "Shall we read it together?"

Caris handed the letter over and took a seat, her hands clasped on her knees. "Every time we get one I wonder if it'll be that letter. The one that takes them away from us."

Cadoc snorted. "I don't think you have anything to worry about. It's been five years and I think they would kick and scream bloody murder if we tried to send them to America now."

Her lips thinned in acknowledgment and she let out a sharp breath. "But she's their mother. I'm not. Even though I've had the raising of them the last five years, she could send for them at any time."

"We've had the raising of them together. And as I said, I don't think you have anything to worry about."

Cadoc unfolded the letter and scanned the contents before he raised his head in disbelief. "She's not asking for them."

Caris wrung her hands in her lap. "She wants us to bring them? Or she's coming home to retrieve them?"

He shook his head. "Neither." He broke into a smile. "She's relinquishing them to our care. Permanently."

His sister's mouth flew open in astonishment. "Truly?" She asked as she leapt up and twirled around. The news clearly made her giddy.

"Truly," he said as he extended the letter in her direction.

She took it and read it even faster than he had. "Gwyn writes that they are headed for the Yukon Territory, and she doesn't know when they'll be in a position to take them. What's in the Yukon Territory?"

Cadoc grimaced. "Gold." Their brother-in-law was stricken with the goldbug and followed it wherever there were rumors of making a quick fortune. He dragged his family back and forth with him, across rough, often inhospitable terrain. Their sister had already lost two children to deprivation and sickness, and Cadoc was glad Davy and Ella would remain in England. Here at least he could ensure they were safe, healthy and well-fed.

"They'll be here, in our care. For good." Caris's eyes shone as brightly as her smile.

Cadoc smiled back. "At least until they're in a profession or wed."

"Pshaw. I'm not going to think about that. I plan to enjoy my relief. I've lived in fear for five years - that they would go across the ocean and I'd never see them again."

# *Chapter Three*

IT HAD BEEN ALMOST three weeks since he'd issued his challenge. Jess had spent every single night in the interim tossing and turning, determined to devise a solution that didn't require her surrender.

She couldn't very well sneak into his house and somehow miraculously retrieve the microscope without being discovered. She refused to give him the satisfaction of an easy conquest, and the situation she found herself in was unconscionable.

That morning, she'd finally decided to confront him and demand he observe the rules of gentlemanly behavior. She took a deep, fortifying breath and set the brass knocker against the heavy oak door. *One. Two. Three.* She could hear the steady thunk reverberating through the hall and wished she was tall enough to see through the peephole installed just above the crown of her head. She was here against her better judgment, determined to persuade him against their bargain. She'd worn her most straightforward ensemble - an unadorned white shirtwaist with plain buttons and a serviceable skirt devoid of bustle.

She was second-guessing the outrage that had spurred her to beard the lion in its den when the door swung open. He leaned against the threshold and stretched one arm above him to grasp the frame.

His unbuttoned shirt swung open and Jess caught a glimpse of dark hair arrowing down his navel before she wrenched her gaze away. Jess had never seen a man's bare chest because most men wore vests under their shirts. For some unknown reason, Cadoc Morgan was contrary and chose not to adhere to custom. She jerked her eyes up from the bead of sweat that was slowly trickling down one exposed pectoral muscle.

Not only was he inappropriately attired, his cheek and forehead were streaked with grease.

He gave her a lazy, insouciant grin. "What brings you to my doorstep, Miss Wainwright?"

"I'm here to appeal to your conscience."

He gestured magnanimously toward the hallway behind him and Jess struggled to ignore how the expansive gesture caused the unmoored shirt to gape at his sides.

"You're welcome to try your luck, and I'll enjoy watching you embark on a futile journey."

When he gave her his back she shut the door. The length of his stride was ground-eating, and she had to scurry to keep up. Like an ignominious rodent. The tails of the shirt fluttered upward as he walked, and Jess caught a glimpse of his back. It was covered with pale scars - a web of them stretched upward from the base of his spine and marred the golden expanse of skin.

She knew nothing of his life before he'd shown up in Heathsted, and she wondered what he was hiding behind his devil-may-care flirtation with her. If his roguish nonchalance was nothing more than a mask. Jess had her own masks, meant to be donned in polite society and to keep those she didn't know at bay.

She thought about what it would feel like to meet this man on his own terms, no masks between them.

The room he led her to was cavernous. Tools, wiring and several glass and metal cylinders were strewn over the large table dominating the center of the room.

"What is this?" Jess asked. She mused privately that it was exactly as she'd pictured Dickens' curiosity shoppe. Full of mystery and hidden corners. Gears and handles and bearings covered every flat surface.

He ignored her question to swipe his cheek with a rag he pulled from his pocket. His efforts did nothing but spread the grease. She wanted to step into the space between them, lick the tip of her finger, and wipe it away. Like she would do for one of the children in first primer. With the grease in his dimple and his hair askew, he resembled one of her mischievous students. She decided to repeat her question. "I asked what this was."

"It's my workshop, Miss Wainwright. You'll have to excuse the hearing in my left ear. All those years in the mine affected it more than the hearing in my right."

Jess stowed away that tidbit of information to mull over later. She tapped her cheek. "You still haven't gotten all the grease."

He shrugged. "No matter. I still don't have the calibrations I need, so there will be more grease on my person before the night is through."

She clasped her hands behind her back and rocked back and forth on her heels. "I'd assumed this was your workshop, given the state of it." She wrinkled her nose for emphasis. "And the spot of grease on your face."

"It bears repeating, Miss Wainwright, that this is my workshop. Sometimes I strip away my vest and shirt so I can do battle with that," Cad pointed to the sandbag suspended from the ceiling in the other corner of the room. "It helps clear my head. However, I'd like to point out that the state of my wardrobe, or lack thereof, is entirely my concern and none of yours. As you well know, none of my gains are ill-gotten. My wealth comes from my inventions and for some unfathomable reason you've interrupted the solitude I require to perfect my latest contraption. I should ask you to excuse the grease, but I won't, because your visit is unexpected."

She folded her arms at her waist and steadfastly ignored the gaping shirt. "I've thought over your proposition, Mr. Morgan. At length. My sister Cecily convinced me to appeal to your sense of propriety and justice. So that is what I've come to do."

He tossed the rag aside and put his hands on his hips. She thought he was going to scold her again until he threw back his head and roared with laughter. "You should know by now that I have no sense of propriety and your little visit isn't about seeking justice. You're here because you're intrigued by my proposition."

He'd stepped closer as he spoke, until he was a handbreadth away.

"Cadoc," she lifted her chin to fume up at him. "I should call you Cad instead. I'm not intrigued. I think you're arrogant and enjoy manipulating circumstances to your satisfaction. No decent gentleman would insist on carrying out such a bargain or answering the door half-clothed. I must insist you button up your shirt."

"I never claimed to be a gentleman. Quite the opposite in fact, Miss Wainwright." He leaned forward and cupped her cheek in his palm and a quiver of excruciating awareness trekked like a lightning bolt from the base of Jess's spine to the tips of her toes. "In fact," he murmured, as his fingers grazed her ear, "My touch would have spread nothin' but coal dust across your face ten years ago."

He moved his hand slowly down her neck, and toyed with the button at her collar. "So prim and proper and wrapped up tight," he muttered underneath his breath, and slid the tip of his finger between fabric and skin. He lightly stroked her collarbone and his touch was a white-hot flame.

"Your cheek would bear the stain of my ungentlemanly hands," he rubbed his knuckle over the button and feathered that diabolical finger over her heart. "Your white shirt would bear the mark of my hand - no matter how diligently you applied yourself to the launderin' of it."

His voice was raw, and she could hear the yearning in it. Jess clenched her fists and hoped he couldn't feel how she trembled at his touch.

"Remove your hand from my personage," she demanded as she tugged his roaming fingers away from her bodice. She couldn't afford to let him crawl beneath her defenses.

He winked and stepped back. "I'm fairly certain I never outlined the terms of our bargain, Miss Wainwright. What leads you to believe your mere appearance is sufficient enticement?"

"I've already explained I am not here to accept your bargain."

He strode toward the window and when he pushed aside the heavy drapery to lean against it,  she tried to ignore the way the sunlight caught the glints in his dark hair, so they looked like a star-strewn deep blue sky. From where she was standing she could see strands of white at his temples, like moonlight.

"What if I made the wager a scientific experiment?"

"It depends on what kind of experiment. Is it a legitimate one or something you're devising to make me even more uncomfortable?"

"For every kiss you allow me to take, and remain unmoved by, I'll return a piece of your microscope to your keeping."

Jess was skeptical. "I only have to endure your advances and you'll give it back to me."

He nodded. "One piece at a time."

Letting him exercise his charms might be her only option and Jess was confident she could resist him. Perhaps she could make her resistance its own experiment. It was simply a matter of letting her mind, rather than the animal instincts he aroused, control her reactions. Objectively, she knew a black heart beat in his chest - as black as the coal from whence he came. His heart was probably exactly that - a black lump of coal. She would use that knowledge to reinforce her resistance.

"I'll agree to your absurd experiment." She steeled herself for his gloating response.

"I think you need time to mull it over."

His reply wasn't the one she'd been bracing herself for.

"You don't even possess the courtesy to start now?" She wasn't prepared for his reluctance. She wanted to get it over with. Prolonged exposure to Cadoc Morgan would weaken her defenses. Like the steady erosion of water over stone.

"No. I'll let you preserve your dignity a while longer. I'm in no hurry and you informed me that you didn't actually need the microscope in the classroom until spring. We've barely begun to feel the first sting of winter."

"What if I mull over your proposal and change my mind about accepting it?"

He shrugged. "Then you change your mind. And lose all hope of getting your microscope back."

"And let you win." Jess wanted to ball up her fist and set it against the irritating corner of his smirk.

"Madam, I win either way," he told her as he crossed his arms and studied her from his perch in the window alcove.

"And I lose either way. You are forcing me to choose between my virtue and my vocation." The rage simmered in her veins.  He was rendering her impotent - when she craved control and independence above all else.

"Do you have an alternative proposal?" He was far too cavalier and nonchalant about the entire situation.

"My sister said I should tell you I need the microscope for my own use - not just for the schoolroom."

"Tell me then, Miss Wainwright."

"For the last five years, I've made an observation of dragonflies in their natural habitat. Their behavior signals the health of a pond, and when they proliferate, it bodes well. When their population dwindles, or the larvae don't survive to adulthood, it's a harbinger of changes in the environment that demand attention. I want to publish my hypotheses and include drawings of the various species I've found."

"Why is your microscope necessary for that?"

"I want my drawings to be accurate."

"Then you should be all the more eager to assume our bargain."

"Your ridiculously manipulative behavior is both importuning me and impeding science."

"No need to sound so lofty, Wainwright. I know exactly what I'm doing. While I appreciate your additional explanation, it doesn't sway me in the least."

"So you'll not be persuaded from your course?"

He slowly shook his head, so his refusal was unmistakable.

Jess felt the weight of it sink into her bones. She couldn't give up the project that had consumed every spare moment of her time. But she was afraid of the wildness that leapt in her heart at the thought of his kisses. What if she couldn't remain unaffected and she made the bargain for naught?

"Fine. I'll give you my decision the night of the pageant. Davy is one of the wise men and Ella is playing the role of Mary, so I know you'll be there."

"I look forward to it."

Jess endeavored not to stomp away. And not to look back.

# Chapter Four

"Miss Wainwright paid a visit?" Caris asked as she came to stand beside him. They watched from the doorway as Jess Wainwright walked down the lane. Her chin was thrust forward and her arms were swinging back and forth so vigorously she could row a boat. Even with her voluminous cape constricting her stride, her aggravation was evident. The knowledge he had provoked her to such levels of agitation made Cadoc smile.

"Yes." He curtly said, irritated by the interruption. Because he wanted to keep his gaze fixed on her until she was nothing more than a speck in the distance. Because he could still feel the fleeting texture of her skin against his palm. Because he wanted to hold onto the glimpse of fire he'd seen in her eyes before she ruthlessly banked it.

"She left without popping in to say hello to Davy and Ella?"

If he turned, he knew her eyes would be narrowed in concentration. And as soon as she saw his expression she'd be able to tell how fascinated he was with their guest. He let the silence build until the object of his fascination disappeared over the rise.

"She wasn't here to speak with Davy and Ella. She was here to speak with me."

Caris chuckled. "I know how you are, big brother. If a lass acts like she wants nothing to do with you, it makes you chase her all the harder. Her departure wasn't exactly swanning about. She seemed angry. Have you been meddling in her life, as you're wont to do when you want something or someone?"

"She thinks I'm a bounder and an ingrate," he sighed. "I'm not chasing her. I'm letting her come to me. I have something she wants."

"Mam always said you were devilish when you wanted something. So attuned to your purpose you're oblivious to the havoc you wreak or the destruction you leave in your wake. Your arrogance will bite you in the arse, some day. Your reach always extended beyond your need. Take care your selfishness isn't going to destroy everything she's built." She wagged her finger at him.

"I know what I'm doing, little sister. And she does too."

"You always say that and I've yet to believe you. I know you have Old Scratch's own luck and his strategy."

"Old Scratch was tossed out of heaven on his arse, little sister. If that's the kind of luck you think I have, it doesn't bode well for me. And strategy is only a matter of taking advantage of inherent weakness."

She lightly punched him in the shoulder. "I meant Satan's penchant for tricking unsuspecting people into doing his bidding. You've always had a way with words, Cadoc, and been able to convince others to do things they seemed dead set against."

"I think Miss Wainwright is made of sterner stuff. She'll stick to her ideals as long as she can."

Caris shook her head in bemusement. "I don't know what you have planned for her, or what sort of devil's bargain you've made, but it's not like you to become tangled up with a woman like this." She reached forward to pinch his forearm. "She has a respected place in this community and she's managed to persuade your niece and nephew to finish their lessons. Don't do something that makes me ashamed to be your sister."

He lifted her fingers one by one. "Surely you think better of me than that."

"I do. But I also know how arrogant you can be and how much you like to win. No matter what game you're playing."

"It's not arrogance. It's recognition that sometimes my mind works faster than everyone else's. She's the only woman I've met in more than a decade who isn't intimidated by that. And who meets me head-on."

"I understand why that would beguile you, because you're not accustomed to it. But you can't destroy her reputation, Cadoc."

"I won't," he growled in frustration. Because he wouldn't. If Miss Wainwright agreed to the wager, he knew she'd be doing it despite her instinct for self-preservation. Because she'd felt the flutter of the thing between them this afternoon as surely as he had. Even if she refused to acknowledge its existence. That was why he didn't believe his actions were reprehensible. "No matter what happens, Caris, I'll watch out for her well-being."

She gave him a sharp nod. "Make sure that you do."

Cadoc was eager to change the subject. The more he dwelt on Jessamine Wainwright, the more he was distracted. "Have you conveyed the news to Davy and Ella yet?"

"I haven't. I thought we could break it to them together over supper tonight. I've made their favorite - rabbit stew and dumplings."

Cadoc grimaced. He would never tell his sister, but somehow the thought of consuming something that had once been frolicking through the meadow in all its fluffy glory, turned his appetite. "Yes, we'll tell them together."

When Davy and Ella were halfway through their second bowls, Cadoc decided it was as good a time as any to let them know about their mother's decision. He cleared his throat. Perhaps the best way to share the news was quickly. "Davy and Ella," he began in a brusque tone. "Yout Aunt Caris and I recently received a letter from your mother."

Davy frowned and laid his spoon on the table. "She never writes to us," he complained.

Ella looked down into her bowl, her expression unreadable. "I don't think she remembers us, Davy," she quietly said.

"I don't think that's true, children," Caris reassured them.

"Then why hasn't she sent for us?"

Cadoc understood his nephew's belligerence. It stemmed from his hurt and feelings of abandonment. The lad had been seven when Gwyn had left with her husband. Old enough to understand his parents were leaving him behind because they thought he would be a burden.

"She and your father haven't been able to provide you with a stable home. She knew if you stayed with us you'd be taken care of."

"But we miss them," Ella wailed.

"We know you do, poppet," Caris laid a hand on her hair to soothe her.

"So what was the letter about? Do they finally want us to come live with them?"

Cadoc steepled his hands together in front of him and leaned forward. "Not precisely."

Davy's face darkened. "She doesn't want us anymore."

The boy was correct in principle. "Your parents are making their way to the Yukon Territory. It is an inhospitable landscape and they think you'll be better off remaining here with your aunt and I."

"So I was right," Davy grumbled into his soup.

"She believes she's making the best decision for your future. You have the opportunity for an education and more hopeful prospects here."

"What about me? Very few girls are permitted to attend university. Miss Wainwright says she doesn't think that will change until we have the right to vote."

"Miss Wainwright is correct. But you've shown promise in your studies, Ella, and you have a lively mind. Do you want to go to university?" Cadoc would use his money and influence to grease the wheels if Ella wanted to pursue her studies.

Ella primly clasped her hands in her lap and lifted her chin. "I think I should like to."

"Then we shall do all we can to ensure you can," Caris said in a brisk tone.

"Will the two of you be alright?" Davy had a thunderous look on his face and was still staring into his bowl.

"I didn't want to go anyway. America's full of nothing but bears."

The boy's hurt was seeping into his words. Cadoc stood and rounded the table so he could lay a hand on his shoulder. "It's perfectly normal to feel the way you're feeling, lad. I know you were excited about the journey across the ocean. And perhaps awed at the prospect of seeing actual cowboys. When your parents are settled in one place, your aunt and I will take you to visit them."

"Promise?" Davy hoarsely asked.

"I promise. I'll do everything in my power to ensure you see them again."

"Thank you, Uncle Cadoc." Ella said in an unnaturally high voice. As if she was holding back the tears as well.

After he and Caris had put them to bed, they met in the library. He poured them both a robust splash of whisky and leaned back in the chair before the fire. He held his glass out. "A toast to that chore being over."

She clinked her glass to his and leaned back in the opposite chair. "They took the news much better than I thought they would," she said.

Cadoc frowned into his glass before he tossed it back. "I don't like seeing them hurt like that."

"Neither do I, brother. But surely you realize it's for the best. They have far more resources at their disposal and more opportunities that are theirs for the taking."

"Do you think Mam would be appalled at the way we've all grown apart? She did everything she could to keep us together after Da died. That's why she went into the pit."

Caris took a hearty sip and thumped her head against the back of her chair. "I think she'd be disappointed that we didn't convince Gwyn to stay. I think she'd be sad that Helen and Mary went to India and that Mary died there. I think she'd be sorry Ellen married a miner."

"Do you think we'd be any different as a family if she and Griffin were here with us?"

"Ahh, brother. Whisky always makes you introspective."

"That's not true. Are you going to answer me or not?" Whisky always seemed to diminish the gap between now and then, and made him look at the choices he'd made with a jaundiced eye. It didn't mean he was overcome with sentimentality.

Caris held out her glass for another dram. After he'd poured it and she took another swig, she whistled through her teeth. "I think you were always in Griffin's shadow. He was so much older than the rest of us. I think if he'd lived, you never would have overcome that. I don't think we'd be here and I don't know that you would've been compelled to start inventing things. Because I know you began working on the first lamp to prevent what happened to them from ever happening again."

Cadoc smiled at the thought of their eldest brother. "'Twas hard not to be in Griffin's shadow. He always dominated whatever space he was in." Griff had possessed a hearty laugh and a healthy dose of humor that permeated his surroundings. "There was always a jest on his mind or a bawdy song on the tip of his tongue, and he never exercised restraint in giving voice to either."

"Remember when one of his mates dared him to compose an englyn and recite it at the eisteddfod?"

"How could I forget? He practiced day and night. Muttering under his breath no matter what he was doing. He nearly won too, even though he'd never written a poem in his life until then."

Caris's expression grew wistful. "Mam was so proud of him."

"She was. We all were. The other drammers ribbed me constantly, but I knew they were secretly envious and impressed."

"I can still see him standing on the dais with his hands folded behind his back and his legs braced apart. It took him so long to begin speaking, we worried he'd forgotten it."

"And then the penfyr he'd been composing just rolled off his tongue and we were awestruck. Like the poetry had been lying dormant in his soul. *Deep in the mine, scarce and slow the sunlight, that creeps with a glow and shines, a mirror to the divine."* As soon as he'd begun reciting, his sister's voice entwined with his. The words echoed through the room, a solemn reminder of the bonds that had held them together when there was scant light in their lives.

"I'd forgotten how beautiful his poem was. How I couldn't explain my tears after I heard it."

"His nickname was Bard after that, because his words captured what we all felt when we climbed the shaft and felt the sun on our faces. It was always like seeing the face of God after you'd forgotten how the radiance of it could wipe everything away."

"The mine took him too soon. Even as it was putting bread on our table, it took it away. It took so much away from us and the other families in the valley. I always wondered why you never made competing in the eisteddfod a tradition."

Cadoc shook his head. "I was too much of a pragmatist. The way the metal and the cogs and gears felt in my hands, I knew that's how I would change things. Griffin's voice was the longing for something, and I was made to be the doing of it."

The fire from the hearth made the room warm and cozy, lulling them both to contemplative silence.

"I don't think I'll ever forget the look on your face when you came to the cottage to tell us the news." Caris's voice was soft and full of pain. "You were shaking and could barely stand because you ran the whole two miles. And your eyes, Cadoc. I knew before you said the words that the terrible noise I'd heard meant sorrow for our family."

"I had to get to you before anyone else. I had to be the one to tell you they were gone."

Caris rose and knelt before him. His grip was white-knuckled on the arm of the chair, and he could feel the brutal press of the glass beneath his other palm. She peeled his fingers from both, set the glass on the floor and clasped his hands. "I know how hard it was, brother, to become Da and the both of them to us. You sacrificed so much that day, and you were never the same. I know you carry that burden with you, that guilt that you were replacing them instead of honoring them."

Cadoc turned a red-rimmed gaze to her. "How could you possibly know that?" He gruffly asked.

Her smile was gentle. "Because I know you, brother. Because I see the parts of our past, the ones that made us who we are, that you try to hide. I think that's why you're pursuing the schoolmistress. She reminds you of something you thought you'd lost forever."

He suddenly knew she was right, and it was like an anvil had lifted from his chest. In moments like this, his sister's insight never failed to render him speechless. He blinked back the tears.

She patted his hand one last time and rose. In that moment, she looked so much like their mother he wanted to howl and thrash his fists and weep. "I'll leave you to your whisky and your meandering thoughts, brother. Please think on what I've said and come to terms with why winning whatever wager you've made with Miss Wainwright is so important to you."

After Caris had slipped from the room, Cadoc stared into the fire again. When he closed his eyes, he could relive that moment when he knew he'd never see their faces again and he would be the one to tell his sisters. The anvil was lifted now, but he could still feel the ghost of its crushing weight pinning him in place, like a bird shot down with an arrow through its wing. He ruefully acknowledged his sister's wisdom.

Jess Wainwright lifted the weight of that anvil from his soul, and that's why he was so hellbent on making her his. When he looked into her eyes, he saw the same shadows and old sorrows that cloaked him. Those shadows resonated with his own. Even if he achieved his ends dishonorably, and he didn't make her his for longer than the next morning, he could no longer deny the irrefutable truth of what her surrender would mean.

# *Chapter Five*

“I FIND MYSELF IN a predicament.”

Vin’s head popped around the side of the pantry door. She’d recently proclaimed it was her new simples room - as if she were some medieval heroine living in a castle instead of a cramped two bedroom cottage with her remaining four unwed sisters.

“Is it a predicament that requires poison?”

Jess laughed despite herself. “You seem much too keen at the prospect.”

“I can make it undetectable. There are many ways to disguise it and fell one’s opponents. Or enemies.”

“I admit, that would be an easy solution. Especially since my predicament involves Cadoc Morgan.”

Vin’s expression grew speculative. “The inventor? Isn’t he the superintendent of your school?”

“Yes to both questions.”

"What's he done? In the village they say he's quite the rogue." Her expression darkened with malice. "If he's compromised you, I should poison him."

"He hasn't compromised me - yet."

Vin's brows flew to her hairline. "Yet?" She ominously asked.

"He absconded with my microscope last month. And he won't return it unless I accept the terms of the illicit wager he's proposing."

"Why haven't you gone to the magistrate?"

Jess shook her head. "I can't do that."

Vin's eyes narrowed as she stalked from the doorway with one hand braced on her hip. "Why not?"

"He's threatened to expose you."

"That bloody blackguard polyp on the arse of a goat! He's blackmailing you! Because of me." Her face was dark with fury.

"What you do for the women in this parish is important." Jess took a fortifying breath. "I'll not jeopardize it. Especially since Fran's busy with the practice she and Mac have and can't assist you."

"There has to be something I can do to help. To put the scoundrel in his place."

Jess shook her head in refusal. "Our wager right now consists only of kisses. But I don't trust him, or my own attraction to him, to restrict us. The most I've ever allowed a suitor is heavy petting over my clothes. And even that was repugnant."

"You're worried you'll allow him to seduce you," Vin narrowed her gaze and Jess felt like one of her own dragonfly specimens pinned to the corkboard.

She gulped. "Yes. And if that happens, I don't want consequences. That's why I'm telling you all of this. I may be a scientist and I may know about biology and anatomy and procreation, but this is your field of expertise. I need to hear the entire lecture you give the women of the parish because I want to be armed with all the knowledge available to me."

"I can do that. And I'll provide you with the same contraceptives as well." She turned to wipe her hands on the towel by the dry sink. "We should have it when Gert and Emily are occupied with other things. I know they're both going to London after the holidays. Can you resist him until then?"

"I told him I wouldn't give him my decision until the night of the school pageant. He'll be there because of his niece and nephew." Jess blew out a breath. "I can hold him off until then."

Vin nodded sharply. "That's plenty of time for me to gather what I need. Meanwhile, don't let him waylay you."

"He won't have the opportunity to waylay me. I have far too much on my mind at the moment to allow him to do so."

It was the last day of school before the winter holidays and although the look of the clouds made her uneasy, Jess was determined to stop in the village and purchase the dry goods she needed.

Vin had given her a list and coins that morning, and she had them tucked into the reticule hanging at her waist. The emporium was filled to capacity when the door chimed at her entrance, and Jess took her place at the end of the queue.

"John said he doesn't like the look of the clouds," one of the women ahead of her confided. "He bade me to pick up flour, sugar and salt."

Jess had to strain to hear her over the hubbub, and Mr. Bennett's voice tense when he called the next customer to the counter. "Does your husband think there's a storm on the way?"

"Aye, he said the ache in his knee was telling him 'twould be even worse than the one we had last winter."

The storm last winter had stranded Arie on Thaddeus St. Simon's farm. Arie had finally realized she need not make sacrifices for her sisters and she grasped her chance at happiness. She and Thad wed in the spring and she'd given her sisters a niece to dote on at the beginning of September.

Fran had delivered the babe using a method she'd called Caesarean, and she and her new husband Mac had stayed long enough to make sure the mother and child were well before returning to London. Fran had sent word via telegram last week they'd be coming home for Christmas. The only sister who wouldn't be joining them was Cece. Her most recent letter had been addressed to all of them and she'd informed them of her decision to remain in Scotland for the holidays. Jess would sorely miss Cece's sympathy and willing ears. Even if her youngest sister couldn't solve her dilemma, her gentle words were like a balm and eased the heart.

The bell chimed behind her, just as Jess was going to ask her chatty companion if her husband had any further predictions. She felt a familiar prickle at her nape and knew who had just entered the mercantile.

"Fancy seeing you here, Miss Wainwright," he rumbled just over her ear.

Jess kept a tight grip on her reticule and let it ground her. She'd managed to avoid him for two weeks, and now she was trapped. If she was rude, it would be observed and commented on. "I think many of us are stocking our larders because of the impending storm."

"Caris sent me here for flour because she has half the household securing the windows and making windbreaks to wedge under the doors."

"See, lass? I told you my John's bones were right. Even the superintendent is preparing for what's coming."

"How fare you, Mrs. Conry?"

He must have moved closer, because Jess swore she could now feel the rumble of his voice through the thick wool of her cloak. She fought the urge to pull up the hood and block the vibrations.

"We fare well, Mr. Morgan. Please accept my thanks once more for your intervention at the mill. John needed Hugh's help to get in the harvest. It would have rotted in the field if you hadn't spoken a sharp word to the millwright about the boy's hours."

"I was glad to be of service, Mrs. Conry," Cadoc said.

The flutter of hair at her nape alerted Jess he'd bowed.

Jess was relieved when only Mrs. Conry stood between her and the harried shopkeeper.

She gave the man a bright smile when she reached the front of the queue. "I need flour and sugar, and two spools of red thread."

"We're out of sugar, Miss Wainwright, and I can only give you five pounds of flour."

"That's fine Mr. Bennett, we can make do with the honey we have left instead."

As the man packaged up her purchases, Cadoc leaned forward again. "I hope you have plenty of coal and blankets, as well, Miss Wainwright."

"Not that it is any of your concern, but yes, we do, Mr. Morgan."

"Just making certain there is something to warm your bed at night," he murmured into her ear.

"You cannot be seen whispering in my ear, Mr. Morgan," Jess whispered back. "It will set the tongues wagging."

"If I convey you to your home, will it cause tongues to wag?"

"You know it will. You are much too forthright in your pursuit. You'll have my answer in one week."

"I am eager to accept your surrender."

"This is not a battle, sir."

"You may delude yourself as long as you like, madam," he countered just as Mr. Bennett slid her packages across the wooden counter.

Jess counted out three pence for her purchase, thanked the shopkeeper, and turned back around. "I shall see you at the chorale, Mr. Morgan."

The sky had darkened to an ominous purplish blue while Jess waited in the mercantile, and a few solitary flakes already danced in the air. She wound her scarf more tightly about her throat and pulled her bonnet firmly over her ears. The breeze was quite brisk and the rain from yesterday was already freezing in patches along the lane.

The cottage she shared with her sisters was less than a quarter of a mile, and her packages were light. Jess could easily avoid the treacherous spots and make it safely home on foot.

She settled her purchases more firmly in her arms and set off. She was halfway home when a mighty gust of wind nearly knocked her to the ground. She struggled against it, lowering her head to hide her eyes from the stinging bits of ice it carried with it.

Her feet were sliding from beneath her before she knew what was happening, and her entire body folded down upon her right ankle. When she struggled to rise to her feet, the ankle refused to obey. She leveraged herself upright again, sweat on her brow, and hobbled to the nearest building, the livery stable, so she could hold onto it and steady herself.

The snow was falling more thickly now. Great white puffs of ice that had already blanketed the road. She was nearly on the outskirts of town, and there wasn't a soul stirring. Dense silence surrounded her, all sound smothered by the storm. Somehow, she would have to make it the last eighth of a mile home, even if she had to do it one throbbing, painful inch at a time.

She'd just mustered the courage to take the first step, when a flashy chestnut horse appeared around the corner. Jess immediately knew to whom it belonged. His head was bowed against the wind, but he sawed on the reins when he came in sight of her.

Cadoc Morgan practically leapt from his horse and led it over to her. "Are you hurt?" He shouted over the eerie howl of the wind.

"My ankle," Jess confessed.

"Your cottage is on my way, I'll make sure you get there safely."

Jess braced herself to step forward, but he must have seen something in her face. He looped his mount's reins over the hitching post and scooped her into his arms. "Obviously I don't have a lady's saddle, so you'll need to grasp the pommel," he said as he lifted her up.

"You needn't escort me home, Mr. Morgan," she protested.

He snorted in obvious amusement. "Then how will you get there, pray tell? You'll be an icicle by the time you reach it and only make your ankle worse. What if you cause irreparable damage? Let me stow your packages in the saddle bags and we'll be off."

Jess watched in disbelief as he gathered all her purchases. He even chased down one of the spools of thread being hurtled pell mell down the lane by a gust of wind. Once he'd secured them all, he grasped the reins firmly in one hand and swung himself up behind her. She could feel the solid warmth of him against her back, and his body became a shield against the wind. When they lurched forward, Jess valiantly fought the urge to grasp his arm.

"I would have made it home," she mumbled from behind her scarf.

"At the risk of what, you obstinate woman? Can't you simply be grateful for my timely rescue?"

"I do not wish to imbalance the scales between us. And though I'm grateful for your rescue, it changes nothing. I am not ready to give you my answer."

"I would not accept it if you tried to do so. When you come to me, Jess Wainwright, I want your eyes wide open and your steps without hesitation."

"You seem confident of the outcome, Mr. Morgan."

"I am a hunter of sorts, madam. And I've made certain you have little recourse but to accept my wager."

"My sister Lavinia believes you are the devil incarnate. I've told her of your blackmail threat."

"Given her profession, I should hire a taste tester."

Jess smiled wryly. "She did ask me if I needed her to find a way to poison you."

"I have risen to a place my family should never have risen to, and I've endeavored to stick to my principles while doing it. Your sister isn't the first person to want my demise."

"She's quite adept. You should tread carefully. Perhaps you can simply drop me at the door instead of risking the chance of stirring her wrath."

"You shouldn't put weight on your ankle, and we are nearly there." His arm grazed her cheek as he raised it to point out how close they were.

Jess could barely make out the cottage through the swirling snow. There was no sign of the rooster, who was usually perched on the gate no matter the weather. He had a tendency to peck at the heels of strangers and was a superb guardian.

When they stopped at the gate, he looped the reins over the newel post and dismounted first.

He raised his arms. "I'll catch you."

Jess closed her eyes and slid quite ungraciously into his embrace. He caught her, and when she would have slipped away, his hand slid to her hip. "No. You'll allow me to carry you."

"I know resistance is futile," she said as she rolled her eyes.

This time, when he lifted her into his arms, Jess was determined to focus on some point in the distance instead of stealing a glance at his profile. She could feel the rise and fall of his muscled chest against her side, and the image of it naked and covered in a sheen of sweat and his ridiculously open shirt flashed through her brain. She laced her hands behind his neck and faced resolutely forward.

# Chapter Six

CADOC WANTED TO LAUGH at the obstinacy of the woman in his arms. He'd heard the hitch in her breath when he set his hands on her waist. She was far from impervious to his touch. The curtains in the front window fluttered, and before he could knock, the door was flung open.

"What did you do to her?" Lavinia Wainwright demanded.

"She twisted her ankle on the icy road, and I was kind enough to bring her home."

Lavinia scowled up at them. "Were you following her, you brigand?"

"Vin, stop. Loathe as I am to admit it, I don't think I would have made it home without his assistance."

The sisters exchanged a look. Vin's face finally softened, likely because she saw the lines of exhaustion and pain etched into Jess's expression.

"Your sister was determined to endure the pain and walk home by herself after her injury. I found her clinging to the livery stable on the outskirts of town."

Jess grimaced. "You may set me down now. You've seen me safely home and can be on your way."

"Your ankle needs to be tended. And it should be elevated." Cadoc turned to Vin. "Where can I lay your sister?"

"She has the attic room. Follow me."

Cadoc repressed the urge to take in every detail of Jess Wainwright's life. Her cottage reminded him of the one he'd grown up in, cramped but cozy. He imagined the laughter of she and her sisters soaring to the rafters. A laughter he'd imperiled when he'd threatened to expose her sister Lavinia.

He had to duck his head when they ascended the narrow staircase, or else risk bashing in his skull.

The room at the top of the stairs was sparse. There was a writing desk in the front of the window, a chest at the foot of the wrought iron bed, and a small bookcase. Cadoc ruthlessly squelched the itch to explore everything in her space, especially her bookcase. Getting an intimate glimpse of her inner life was humbling. And made him question his disreputable approach anew.

"You can set me down now," she said in an imperious tone.

Vin stepped aside as he lowered her to the bed and crouched, taking her right ankle in his hand. He deftly unlaced her boot and eased it off.

"Vin could have removed my shoe."

"Yes, Vin could have removed her shoe," Vin sarcastically echoed. "Vin can also remove your head if she thinks you're taking liberties."

"There's no reason for either of you to be so cross," he said over his shoulder. "I needed to see for myself how badly it was sprained. I was going to ride for the doctor if his intervention was warranted."

"Is it bad? We have chorale practice in three days."

"It looks like three or four days of rest will alleviate the swelling. But you'll need to bind it until it heals completely. For at least two weeks."

"Have you had medical training, Mr. Morgan?" Vin interrupted.

"No. I've just seen my share of injuries, both mild and tragic, in the mines."

"So we needn't call for the doctor?" She asked with an expression of trepidation.

Cadoc suspected they could ill afford the expense. "No you needn't. It should heal quickly as long as you stay off that foot." He curled his hand over hers and the feeling of intimacy intruded again. Like a pang in his chest. "But if you'd needed a physician's care, the cost would have been at my expense."

Vin harrumphed behind him. "We don't need your charity, and I'm not inclined to accept anything from you, Mr. Morgan."

"It's not charity," he protested as he locked eyes with Jess. "I feel responsible. If I hadn't goaded you, you might not have been in such a hurry to get home." He wanted his reassurance to stand for more than his offer to pay for a physician. He wanted it to be an apology as well. An abbreviated, premature one, because she still hadn't agreed to the wager, but an apology nonetheless.

"Believe me, Mr. Morgan, you did not rile me. The road was slick and I fell. And my sister is correct, we don't need your charity."

Her rebuff felt like a fist to his gut. He supposed it was no more than he deserved for his high-handed treatment of her the last few weeks. "I would have helped however I could," he gruffly insisted.

"Be that as it may, I can care for my sister from this point forward. We've received a letter from Scotland I'd like to share. Can you see yourself out without banging your head, Mr. Morgan?"

"Yes. I bid you both good day," he gave them an exaggerated bow and made a swift exit.

Bacchus was standing exactly where Cadoc had left him, his chestnut coat covered in snow. He stroked his muzzle. "I'm sorry old boy, not much further."

The snow was nearly blinding and Cadoc sighed in relief when he saw the giant oak that stood at the end of the lane. His home was less than two hundred feet away.

When the stable came into view, the head groom rushed out. "No need, George. I've got him. I'll give him a rubdown and some oats while you tuck into the supper you likely have ready to go."

The bandy-legged man gave him a gap-toothed smile. He was a former miner like Cad, and he'd been like a father figure. When one of the drays crushed his foot and he was confined to a bed for weeks until he could make his way about again, Cad took care of him in return. All of George's family was gone - taken by disease or the mine - and he lost the lease on his cottage. Cad and his sisters had made room for him in their cottage.

The man had always had a way with the dray horses, so when they moved to Cumbria, Cad asked George to accompany them as the new head groom.

"Right you are, young lad. I have a bowl of stew and some fresh bread," George rubbed his stomach to illustrate. "This weather's for neither man nor beast."

"If you're going up to the house, will you let Caris know I'm home and I'll be in shortly?"

"Aye. Don't tarry overlong, the stew may be gone by the time you finish."

After he'd tucked Bacchus in with a bucket of oats, he made his way up the steps. The storm was in full, blinding swing, and the outline of the house in the distance was nearly obscured by the snow. He sighed in relief when he shut the door behind him and stamped and shook the flakes from his coat and boots.

He left his footwear to dry by the door and crept to the kitchen in stockinged feet. When the household was settling in for a storm like this one, they all tended to gather there, in front of the giant hearth. He heard the laughter before he saw them.

He rounded the corner and leapt into a crouch, growling as loudly and disturbingly as he could. Ella and Caris's screams were most gratifying.

"Cadoc, you gave us a fright!" His sister chastised with bright eyes. "Come, have a seat and a bowl of stew. I've kept it warm for you."

Caris was very fond of the wood cookstove he'd bought her when they moved into Heathsted, and delighted in using it.

"Will we be able to take the sled out tomorrow, Uncle?" Davy eagerly asked.

Cadoc regarded him over his spoonful of soup. "If 'tis not too cold, and the visibility is better, I don't see why not. The snow is so dense I could have lost my way between here and the stable and staggered into the woods. You would have found my bones in the spring."

Ella's eyes widened. "You would have turned into a ghost, Uncle? Like Marley from the story you read us?"

Cadoc curled his hands into claws and crossed his eyes in her direction. "Exactly like Marley. I would have haunted you."

She squealed and ducked her head against Caris's shoulder. Caris stroked her hair and glowered at him. "When she has nightmares because of your teasing, you'll be the one to brave the cold floorboards and comfort her."

"Ella, look at me."

"I don't want to, Uncle," she protested and burrowed her head further into Caris's armpit.

"I was only teasing. If there are ghosts, they have more important things to occupy their time. Like figuring out how to get to heaven."

She lifted her head. "Not everyone goes to heaven when they die?"

"The vicar will tell you that only those who've been baptized get past the pearly gates."

"Is that what you think too?"

"I think that if you're good, and you treat others the way you want to be treated, there's a place for you in heaven. Whether or not you've been baptised."

"Blasphemous," his sister muttered with a smile. And then she wagged a finger in his direction. He knew she was scolding him for his treatment of the teacher. Because such treatment was far from a reflection of the tenet he'd just espoused.

"Your teacher has a sprained ankle," he confided to the table at large. "I rescued her and took her home on Bacchus."

"I don't have to be a wise man now?" Davy could barely contain his excitement at the prospect of the pageant being cancelled.

Cadoc ignored Caris's raised brow.

"It's only a sprain," he said to Davy. "She'll be good as new in a few days. I am going to try and find the crutches your aunt Ellen used when she twisted her knee."

At the age of twenty-seven Ellen had decided it was time she conquered her fear of heights. Her solution had been allowing Davy to teach her to climb trees. She'd become dizzy when she crawled out on one of the limbs and lost her grip. She'd been lucky her fall wasn't from a great distance and a sprained wrist and twisted knee were the only disastrous outcomes of her escapade. She'd recuperated with the aid of the crutches, and informed Caris and Cadoc that tree-climbing would not be one of the lessons she delivered as a governess.

"I saw them in the attic!" Davy volunteered. "May I come with you when you go up there to retrieve them?"

Like all children who dreamt of maps to pirate treasure and chests full of long forgotten toys, Davy was fascinated by the jumble of furniture in the attic. "Yes, you may accompany me both to the attic and to Mrs. Wainwright's home when we take them to her."

"If they've been in the attic, you won't dare take them to her without allowing me to give them a good cleaning first."

Cadoc nodded in agreement, because he knew better than to argue with his sister about household things. She was like their mother had been - if she wasn't doing it or showing someone else how to do it the way she'd been taught, it wasn't being done right.

"Can I come with you when you go see Miss Wainwright?"

No one in possession of a heart could say no to Ella's woeful gaze. "You may come if you bundle up. That means mittens, hat, scarf, and your flannels."

Ella complained about the long flannel pantaloons Caris forced her to wear under her skirts in the winter. She said it made her itch and peeled them off at every opportunity. "Fine," she mumbled.

Cadoc quelled his grin at her mutinous expression because he didn't want to hurt her tender feelings. "Then you are welcome to ride along as well."

"But I don't wanna go up in the attic with you. There's a headless man up there."

"A headless man?" Cadoc pinned his squirming nephew with a stern look.

"There's a dressmaker's form stashed in one of the far corners," Caris explained.

Cad turned back to Davy. "And you told her it was a headless man? What have I told you about reading *The Legends of Sleepy Hollow*, Davy? And scaring your younger sister with them?"

"It's not real," Davy flushed and protested.

"Then how would you like to spend the night locked in that room by yourself?" Cadoc would never subject the boy to terror like that, but his teasing of Ella could be mean-spirited, and he needed to fear the repercussions.

"I might be afraid of the headless man, but Davy's afraid of spiders," Ella volunteered. "He wouldn't touch it and then he ran away when Miss Wainwright tried to bring it closer."

"Perhaps wielding the broom in the corners of the pantry for your aunt would be a more fitting punishment."

Davy visibly blanched. "I promise to stop teasing Ella," he vowed.

Caris lifted her hand to cover a smile. Cadoc was finding it just as difficult to keep a straight face.

"I shall hold you to your promise, Davy. Since you and your sister demolished the lemon meringue, you may be excused."

Ella yawned, as if on cue. She stopped at the head of the table on her way upstairs and grabbed his hand. "Uncle Cadoc, will you read one of the fairytales to us tonight?"

He patted her head. "Of course, poppet. Have Nurse put you in your nightclothes and I'll be up shortly."

As soon as the children were out of hearing distance, Cadoc and Caris both erupted into laughter.

"He was terrified," Caris gasped between gusts of amusement.

"He needs to stop tormenting Ella. Perhaps the threat of arachnids will make that happen."

"I think you've frightened him into compliance, brother."

"One can hope. Ella's nightmares are not inconsequential."

Caris grimaced. "I agree. They only prolong the bedwetting."

Cadoc lifted his glass. "I propose a toast to the end of bedwetting."

"I'd prefer whisky to wine, but I accept your toast."

They shared a look of commiseration over the rims of the goblets and he pondered how Miss Wainwright would handle the sibling situation between Davy and Ella. If he wasn't mistaken, she had as much experience as he did both bearing witness and playing the role of peacemaker.

# Chapter Seven

"WE HAVE A LETTER from Scotland?" Jess excitedly asked as soon as she heard the thud of the front door closing behind her rescuer.

Vin slowly nodded. "Our youngest sister has taken leave of her senses."

"She's likely the most sensible of all of us. What makes you say that?"

"She's getting married. And she sounds smitten."

Jess wrinkled her brow in confusion. "Who is she marrying?"

"The ogre."

"The ogre? You don't mean the Scot who almost packed her right back onto the train?"

"The very one. Now that she's come to know him better, she no longer thinks he's the beast in the story."

Jess sighed. Though she didn't begrudge her sister's newfound happiness, she would sorely miss her calming presence and ready assistance. Cece had a way of soothing away the wounds Jess inflicted on others with her sharp tongue. Jess wasn't intentionally terse, she just grew exasperated by social niceties and the reluctance of others to come out and say what they wanted and what they meant. She was more patient with her sisters, because they'd taught her to temper her impatience, and she knew what to expect from them. She hoped Gertrude was available to help her with the chorale preparations and smooth ruffled feathers.

"Are you convinced she's happy?" Jess couldn't fathom her sister forming such a strong attachment to a man she barely knew.

Vin's gaze became introspective. "I am. We all knew she was at a crossroads in her life. We tried to cajole her out of those black rags for almost ten years, to let go of whatever was holding her back from enjoying life again. She found her next chapter in the wilds of Scotland, and despite the fact we don't understand her decision, we have to respect it. As long as he respects her."

Jess wrinkled her nose. "It sounds like he has a physicality to him." Jess had never found large, rough men attractive. Until Cadoc Morgan. As she'd confessed to Cece, even though he wasn't much taller than she was, his body was that of a man who carried women across thresholds and held demons at bay. And she was trying to put him out of her mind. Men like that had a raw sensuality that was overwhelming and distracted her from her work. She preferred to avoid entanglements with them because she sensed she wouldn't be able to control those entanglements.

"A delicious one," Vin agreed with a gleam in her eye. "I'd like to have been there when she saw what he was hiding beneath his kilt."

"You're incorrigible," Jess scolded through her smile.

"I may be incorrigible, but I am also determined to protect my sisters from the folly of unwise choices. Which brings us to the next order of business - I've procured the items necessary to instruct you on contraception."

"According to the queue in line at Mr. Bennett's, a winter storm is barreling toward us. Your procurement could not have come at a more opportune time."

Vin gave her a smug smile. "Not only do we have the opportunity, 'tis better to have this discussion sooner rather than later. The way he looks at you is unmistakable, and you're terribly prickly around him. Which means you're aroused by him as well - even if it's against your better judgment."

Jess cleared her throat and tried to appear nonchalant. "I know he's attracted to me. He's said as much. But I'm as interchangeable as the next woman. The man could charm the fangs from a cobra. He's handsome, and bedsport is likely something he excels at. If this seduction is something I agree to, why shouldn't my deflowering be enjoyable?"

Her sister raised a hand, her face alight with laughter. "I wasn't shaming you, sister. I'm here to ensure your dalliance, if there is to be one, is without consequences. I'll fetch us some tea."

As her sister walked away, Jess pondered the way it had felt to be swept into Cadoc Morgan's arms. Like she was weightless. His chest had been like a steel drum beneath her head, and the steady beat of his heart had been soothing. The arms that had encircled her had been hard too. Lean with muscle.

She thought back to his lewd proposition. When she closed her eyes she could see the swing of his shirt when he answered the door, and the way his bared forearm had looked stretched above his head.

The promise of all that banked strength wrapped so effortlessly around her, and the gentle way he'd lain her down upon this very bed made her stomach flutter.

A clatter at the top of the stairs, and Vin's muttered, "Blast!" snapped her from her musings. It was dangerous to become entranced by Cadoc Morgan.

The rattling teacups preceded her sister into the room. "I dropped one of the spoons at the top of the stairs," she said. "I hope you don't mind sharing one."

So that's what the noise had been. Jess bit her lip so she wouldn't smile. Vin could mix vials, powders and potions with uncanny precision, but she was the clumsiest of her sisters when she wasn't behind an apothecary's counter.

Jess stirred a drop of honey into her tea and waited for her sister to speak.

"I think you should insist he wear a condom. I've procured some for you, but if the rumors are true about his sexual regimen, he probably already has one at his disposal."

"If it comes to that, will I be expected to put it on?"

Vin's grin was vivacious. "That might be titillating, but I think it depends on what his proclivities are."

Jess grimaced. "His proclivity seems to be me. However he can have me. He's like a bloodhound that has the scent of a fox and won't give up the hunt. Or one of those tenacious Bow Street Runners."

"If he wants you that badly, he'll cater to your desires. Make it very clear from the onset you're not letting his jolly roger anywhere near your quim unless it's suited up."

Vin's crudity made her want to laugh, even as she flushed with embarrassment. "You could use the scientific names, you know."

Her sister lifted one shoulder in a very continental expression of indifference. "I could, but why would I? Making you squirm is so much fun. I can see why Morgan enjoys teasing you."

"Fine. I won't let his jolly roger anywhere near my quim unless he's suited up."

Vin's smile turned into a chuckle, and then a boisterous laugh, until she was bent in half, wheezing and clutching her stomach.

"I used your dreadful words, what are you laughing at?"

"Your face..." Vin wheezed. "It looked like you'd just swallowed an unripe slice of persimmon. If you're going to allow him to seduce you, you might want to practice wiping that expression from your face. You'll make him feel like nothing more than a naughty schoolboy."

Jess quirked a brow. "Aren't most men nothing more than naughty schoolboys?"

"Yes, but they don't like to be reminded of their immaturity."

"I'll try and eschew showing my judgment."

"He's probably already aware you don't condone his behavior. From what I hear, he prefers vivacious widows. You're a novelty, so maybe he'll enjoy being scolded."

Jess sincerely doubted Cadoc Morgan let anyone scold him. It would be a blow to his ego, she thought as she emptied her tea.

***

By the time Sunday morning arrived, both Jess and Vin were in need of fresh air and space. The snow was still piled in drifts along the lane, but the air didn't snap with the same frigid bite that had kept them indoors for four days.

As Jess buttoned her claret walking dress, she wondered if the Morgan clan would show up for the service.

The children and Cadoc's sister Caris were always seated in the front pew, but he'd only made a single appearance. The first Sunday after their arrival, he'd sat beside his family. She remembered the tousle of dark hair revealed when he tossed his hat onto the seat beside him, and the way his hands had smoothed the unruly mess behind his ears. He hadn't set foot in the village church since that initial foray.

She pinched her cheeks in the wavy reflection of the mirror, and told herself it was because she looked wan. He wasn't likely to be in attendance anyway.

"Are you ready?" Vin called up from the foot of the stairs.

"Be right down," Jess called back.

When she descended the stairs five minutes later to pull on her cloak and bonnet, Vin was waiting at the door. She narrowed her eyes. "Is that a new dress?"

"It's one Cece finished for me before she left."

"It suits you. I would have thought you'd save it for the pageant, but maybe you're hoping to see a certain elusive rogue," she slyly pointed out.

Jess was glad her back was turned, because she could feel the prickle of heat that danced over her cheeks. Vin couldn't see her blush. "I wanted to make certain the drape and the fit were as they should be."

Vin snorted. "As you say, Jess."

The squat stone of the village church stood impervious to the snow. The trees that cast shade over the cemetery in the summer were ethereal with ice, but the steps and path had been swept meticulously clean.

The hubbub surrounded them as soon as they crossed the threshold. Their pew was near the middle, too far from the lit braziers to feel the heat, so they slid into their seats still bundled beneath their cloaks.

Jess's glance went unerringly to the front of the aisle. She breathed a sigh of relief when she realized he wasn't in attendance. Caris, Davy and Ella were already seated, their heads bent over their hymnals. She pulled off her mittens and was untying her bonnet to set it on the bench beside her when the heavy oak door of the chapel swung open and shut. A chilly breeze stole in, and Jess was tempted to sit on her now bare hands.

And then she heard him. Just as she had in her schoolroom. This time he was muttering apologies for his late arrival to those he passed. His apologies were ridiculous. He wasn't late - the vicar was still conferring with the organist, Mrs. Blevins, and had yet to make his way to the pulpit.

She looked steadfastly ahead and ignored the urge to glance sideways when she felt his eyes on her as he passed. His sudden devotion to tradition was likely a ploy to redeem his notoriety - he was a mere dilettante and had probably never cracked open a bible.

She watched as he unwound the dark blue scarf from around his neck, and remembered with acute clarity the sheen of sweat that had caressed his jawline when he'd answered the door.

# Chapter Eight

HE COULDN'T RESIST SCRUTINIZING her profile as he passed. Her chin was thrust defiantly in the air, her hands clasped tightly in her lap. He wondered if the air around her vibrated, like Dalton's particles, when he was near. Her mere presence made his throat close until it felt like he was trying to breathe through the coal dust again.

Caris gave him an impish sideways look when he slid onto the bench beside her. "Do you have sins you need to repent, brother?" She murmured.

He studied her pointed smile before he replied. "Do you think I have sins I need to repent, sister?"

"I didn't witness it, but I'd wager your gaze lingered on her. You covet, and that is a sin."

Cadoc leaned close to whisper in her ear. "She is not my neighbor's property, and that's all the commandment applies to. I am free to covet and need not confess it."

"Paul equates it with immorality and impurity."

"Leave off your infernal teasing, Caris. I have nothing to confess."

Thankfully the opening chords of the liturgy swelled from the organ and drowned her response.

The sermon that followed the opening prayer made Cadoc squirm in his seat and tap his foot. When the vicar spent a hearty quarter of an hour quoting scripture about lechery, Cadoc felt as if he was the object of the man's proselytization. He might be a man with robust sexual appetites, but he was not a lecher. If the sermon was meant to amend his course, it failed miserably. Cadoc felt no guilt whatsoever about his past or his designs on the village schoolteacher.

He rolled his neck and shoulders in relief when the vicar motioned for the congregation to stand for the closing prayer. "If I ever again have the inclination to attend a Sunday morning service, please dissuade me," he muttered beneath his breath.

Caris chuckled softly. "I know you chafe at conformity, brother."

The prayer ended in the preacher's typical long-winded salutation, and the parishioners began filing into the aisle. Cadoc felt a tug on his fingers, and when he looked back, Ella was beaming up at him. "May we greet Miss Wainwright, Uncle?"

Since Ella's request aligned with his own, he nodded his acquiescence.

Davy and Ella scampered ahead of him and Caris, nimbly weaving their way through the crowd. They caught up to Miss Wainwright just as she descended the stairs.

Cadoc was in earshot when Ella grabbed her skirt and said, "Our uncle said you were hurt during the storm, will you still be able to teach us about spiders and grasshoppers after the holidays? We brought our Aunt Ellen's old crutches for you." His niece pointed vaguely in the direction of their carriage.

She crouched and took his niece's hand in her own. "My ankle is almost completely healed, thank you for asking." Her gaze flicked to his as he drew near. "Your uncle was quite chivalrous to escort me home when I turned it."

Davy sidled closer. "Miss Wainwright, do I have to study the spiders?"

Cadoc smiled at the reticence of his usually exuberant nephew. He was truly terrified of arachnids.

"Davy, you needn't touch them, but the arachnid family has much to teach us."

"As long as I don't have to touch them," he grudgingly conceded.

"But if he examines them more closely, perhaps he'll grow so accustomed to them he no longer fears them."

Jess rose to her feet at his interruption and nodded in his direction. "Mr. Morgan."

He returned her nod. "Miss Wainwright. Do you disagree with my assessment?"

"I know many people who are afraid of spiders, Mr. Morgan. Including several grown men. I think the general feeling of trepidation stems from the cannibalistic reputation of the black widow."

"Will spiders be a part of the holiday pageant, Miss Wainwright?"

"Not intentionally. I'm certain they were present in the corners of the nativity stable, but we won't refer to them in our portrayal of the events."

Davy huffed a sigh of relief at her side.

"I look forward to seeing the play, Miss Wainwright. My niece and nephew are so excited they can talk of little else."

"That's not true, brother," Caris said as she placed her hand in the crook of his arm. "They're very excited to see their Welsh cousins."

"Will you be journeying to Wales for the holiday?"

Jess addressed Caris, but he knew the question encompassed all of them. He wondered if she was trying to wriggle her way out of their agreement.

"Caris, Ella and Davy will be traveling there by train the morning after the play. I'll remain in Heathsted."

She wrinkled her brow at his response, as if he'd flummoxed her.

"If you'll be alone for the holidays, Mr. Morgan, you should join us for Christmas supper."

Jess Wainwright threw a stern look at her sister, and he had no doubt a pinch would have followed if she could have made it unnoticeable. "I'm sure Mr. Morgan has other plans."

He lifted his timepiece as if he was pondering something before he stuck it back in the pocket of his waistcoat. "Actually, I don't have any plans. I'm happy to accept your invitation," he said with a slight bow.

Cadoc wanted to laugh at the teacher's answering grimace. If the decision had been hers, she would have happily let him molder away by himself for the duration of the festivities. When Caris tugged insistently on his arm, he gave the two women a perfunctory bow. "My sister has preparations to make for her extended visit to our family, so I shall bid you adieu. My gratitude once again for the kind invitation to sup at your table."

"We shall see you at three o'clock sharp, Mr. Morgan. And keep in mind that the Wainwrights value punctuality. Especially my sister, Jess," Vin said as she threw her arm around her sister's shoulder.

As Caris pulled him toward their carriage he raised his hand in farewell.

❖

"What possessed you to invite him to our home?" Jess asked, incensed by her sister's meddling.

Vin laughed gaily. "My motives were purely selfish. I want to sit back and watch the drama play out between you."

This time Jess did pinch her sister's arm. "You're supposed to help ward me against him, not give him more opportunities to infiltrate my defenses."

"He won't dare importune you when you're surrounded by family. But I think he'll try imbalancing you - and that's what I want to see. Because I have confidence you'll give as good as you get, sister."

"If he does manage to importune me, I'm holding you responsible."

Vin beamed mischievously. "It will be just like our childhood, Jess. Arie always blamed you for my shenanigans."

"Not always. I could just never prove you were the one at fault," Jess grumbled.

# Chapter Nine

Gert and Emily's train had arrived at the platform three hours ago, and the cottage was full of chatter. Vin had laughingly told them about the plans for Christmas day, and joked about the way Jess constantly complained about the rakish superintendent. When Jess threw her a warning look, Vin simply winked.

The three of them were bent over a London paper Gert had pulled from her valise with a flourish. "I found a press!" she'd called in excitement when she walked through the door.

Gert, Emily and Vin had always been Porthos, Athos and Aramis - the Three Musketeers. And when they were huddled together, it was to the exclusion of their younger sisters Jess and Cece. Her nerves were already on edge about giving Cadoc Morgan her decision tonight, and she didn't know if she could endure their teasing.

When Jess slipped away with a rueful smile and a half-hearted wave, they didn't even acknowledge her departure.

She pulled on her cloak and bonnet from the hook by the door, and trudged outside.

The vicar and the curate were both in the vestibule when she arrived, and Mrs. Blevins was already seated behind her organ. As if she'd never left.

"Ah, Miss Wainwright," the vicar greeted her with an extended hand. "We were just speaking of you. We've sent two of your older students to fetch the backdrop."

Jess dipped a curtsey in his direction. "My sincerest thanks."

The backdrop was a large piece of tarp she and the students had painted. The donkey and the cow looked like non-descript blobs with spindly legs, and the manger definitely resembled a feed trough. But the students had been enthusiastic and proud of their work, so it would serve as it was intended.

One of her curls had escaped the snood, and she tucked it carefully back into the netting.

She wondered idly if he would be punctual, or if he'd make a brash entrance at the very last minute and steal all the air and attention.

When Caris brought Davy and Ella into the vestibule, he wasn't with them.

"Is your brother here?" She casually asked.

Caris frowned. "Ugh, not yet. He's been working in his lab all day. It's his fault I had to scramble to reattach the hem of Ella's robe. Cadoc told them they could bring their puppy in the house to play and the rascal chewed up everything he could reach."

"He's not coming?" Jess hoped Caris didn't hear the disappointment.

Caris tipped her head to the side and flashed Jess a sly grin. "Oh, he'll be here. I know there's something brewing between the two of you."

"We have a reluctant wager, and the stakes are high if I lose."

"I told him to be careful of your reputation and reminded him there are far more rules here about what constitutes proper behavior than there were in the coal mine."

"I know I can't let him turn my head, that I need to stand firm no matter what underhanded tactics he employs."

"Good. It's been a long time since my brother had to fight for something he wants."

"You think I'm the thing he wants?" Jess asked in disbelief. Jess was confident of her appeal, but she was a far cry from the sort of woman he usually consorted with. More prim, more keenly aware of the threat of censure and cautious because of it.

"You're exactly what he wants. I think you're what he needs as well. I'll rest easy on my journey knowing he has somewhere he can go for his Christmas supper."

"Courtesy of my meddling sister."

Caris chuckled. "Your resistance is good for him. Thank you for not retracting the invitation."

"As much as I loathe his manipulation, I wouldn't do that. No one should be alone on Christmas Day."

His sister's expression was grateful. "I agree. I was worried about him, and now I'm not. Please don't hesitate to let me know if I can ever return the favor." She patted Jess's arm as she left the vestibule.

Jess watched her go. The strength of the bond between Caris and Cadoc surprised her. And so did the fierce protectiveness the other woman had shown toward her enigmatic brother. She blinked thoughts of him away and turned to focus on the throng of children.

She clapped her hands together smartly. The conversation came to a halt and all eyes flickered in her direction. "Finish donning your costumes. We're expected in the atrium in a quarter of an hour."

The production was nearly flawless. One of the shepherds lost his supper in the empty manger, and all the other children had simultaneously said "Eww!" and wrinkled their noses, and an angel tripped on her robe and fell into the haystack. The children had recovered from those mishaps like a professional troupe, and she was proud of them.

She could feel Cadoc Morgan's eyes on her as she exchanged niceties with the parents.

# Chapter Ten

CADOC WATCHED HER FLUSH and shake the hands of congratulatory parents. Seeing her, and finally hearing her decision about the wager, was the only thing that had the power to wrench him away from his latest modification. He'd simmered for nearly half an hour as he watched other men's eyes linger on her decolletage. He'd simmered as he watched the sweep of her skirts when she curtseyed. He'd simmered as he watched her hair escape its pins and trail errantly, temptingly down the side of her throat, one lock at a time.

Whenever her gaze turned in his direction, she looked at some point over his shoulder, studiously avoiding meeting his eyes. Even though she knew what he was waiting for. She'd promised to give him her decision tonight, and if he had to, he would wait until every other person took their leavetaking and it was down to just the two of them. So she'd have to look at him and acknowledge him and give him the answer he'd been anticipating for weeks.

When Caris had asked if he'd be accompanying her and the children back to their home he'd told her to proceed without him.

She'd given him a stern look and said, "I know what you're about, Cadoc Elwes Morgan. Keep in mind what I've told you about manipulating her and the repercussions your stalking will have on her life."

The thud of the door and the swirl of snow that landed softly on her face interrupted his reverie. It was finally just the two of them. He was half hidden in the shadows of the corner by the coat room, and he smiled wickedly as he waited for her to notice.

Her purposeful stride brought her within a hands length before she gasped. "You're still here."

He uncrossed his arms. "Where else would I be? I've been patiently awaiting your decision."

"The answer is yes. I'll accept your wager because you leave me no choice." She haughtily brushed past him.

Cadoc was quick on her heels. If she was agreeing to the wager, it began tonight. His grip landed on her wrist as she loosened her grasp on her cloak. "Not so fast, Miss Wainwright. There are things I need to say before we embark on this journey."

She froze beneath his touch, and he was close enough to see the gooseflesh rising at her nape. She was far from immune, no matter how she pretended otherwise or wished to the contrary. "What are you going to do?"

Her voice trembled slightly and he knew she was afraid. He didn't think she was afraid of him - only of her own reaction. He lifted his hand and brushed it over her nape, grazing the knob of her spine, the tendrils of hair, and the flushed skin. She sighed and dipped her head.

Her cloak was twisted in her fingers, as if she thought it would be her salvation. Or her anchor. He would allow it to be neither.

He lowered his head to the place he'd just touched. When he buried his nose in the low bun at her nape he smelled lemon verbena and rosemary. And the subtle tang of her perspiration. Her eyes were closed and he let his lips rest against her delicate skin. "I want your eyes open. No hesitation, Jess Wainwright," he murmured.

"I know what I've agreed to."

"I know you're angry, and you believe I've backed you into a corner. I have. But my intentions in doing so aren't evil."

She snorted. "You may not be pure evil, Cadoc Morgan, but your intentions toward me are wicked. I'm not a fool."

"As I've said, my intentions were never in question. It is your response to them that is in question. Can you resist me, Jess?" He whispered into her ear.

"You haven't earned the familiarity of my given name."

He slid his arm around her, his hand splayed over her ribcage. He could feel the thud of her heart beneath her wool dress, her corset and her chemise. As he pressed closer, her crinoline crumpled and the bell of her skirt swung forward to brush the wall.

"I want to earn that familiarity," he said as he fingered the black ribbon that held her cameo. "I want to earn it," he repeated. If he earned that boon, it would ease the sense of revulsion he felt when he considered what the reprisal to her could be for her surrender. "I never would have exposed your sister. I have sisters of my own and I want them to have choices like those offered by women like Lavinia."

"I thought our wager was for kisses. One at a time. It didn't encompass familiarity. Or heartfelt confessions. How does telling me you made an empty threat improve your case?"

Cadoc smiled at the belligerence in her voice. "There are preludes to kisses, Miss Wainwright, that build the anticipation of the act itself. Until you are aching to feel the supple give of another's mouth beneath your own. Until you want nothing more than to swallow their gasp of surrender."

"So this is a prelude?"

"A prelude. An introduction. The prologue before the main event. Call it what you will, but consider it the stoking of a fire. Until the embers are in danger of leaping from the hearth and charring everything in their path. Especially misgivings and inhibitions."

"I fear it's not just my misgivings and inhibitions that will be incinerated, Mr. Morgan," she softly confessed.

Her admission meant she didn't find him repugnant, that she didn't want a reprieve. He unfastened the clasp of her cameo and twisted the ribbon around his wrist before sliding it into his pocket. Her head fell back, and she rested it against his shoulder. The sweep of her dark lashes fluttered over the lavender crescents just beneath them. She was clearly worn to the bone and the lines of her mouth were lax with either exhaustion or concession. He hoped it was the latter.

If she was finally succumbing to temptation, Cadoc was taking every liberty she'd allow him. He slid his palm around her midriff before he skated it up her ribcage and traced a path around the rise of one breast. Her mouth parted and she moaned. She bit her lip immediately afterward, as if she was quelling her body's betrayal.

The straight arrows of her brows lowered until they nearly touched the bridge of her nose. "This isn't a kiss," she complained.

"No, it's not. It's an experience I want you to agonize over when you're lying in your bed alone."

She shook the hand at her waist free. "I don't want an experience. I agreed to this ridiculous wager because there were clearly defined boundaries. You're crossing them."

"So be it," he muttered and spun her around.

The first flutter of her lips was soft and astonished. Delicate, like the brush of one of her dragonfly wings. When his palm cupped her nape, her hands clutched at empty air before she fisted one of them in his shirt. His kisses were shallow, testing the waters, testing her resolve. Making her question the wisdom of the boundaries she insisted they keep between them.

Cadoc didn't want boundaries or definitions. He wanted this fragile exploration of her awakening. He wanted to watch it bloom like night orchids behind her eyes, and flush her cheeks with ardor she couldn't master or subdue. In his arms, she was everything he'd dreamt she would be.

He coasted his lips over the divot in her chin and the freckles scattered over the bridge of her nose like specks of stardust. He kissed the corners of her eyelids as she closed them, and then the sweep of her lashes and the purple shadows he'd noticed earlier.

His lips weren't a gentle hello the second time. They grazed hers with intention, his hands tangling in her hair until the snood and the bun were gone and the silky mass of curls snuck under his cufflinks and glided over his wrists. He briefly acknowledged he would have welcomed the caress even if she was Medusa and the curls were the tongues of a thousand asps instead. For her, for this kiss, he'd turn to stone.

Her mouth parted again and her muscles tensed beneath his hands. He smothered her protest before she could make it again or push him away. When he slipped his tongue between her lips and slid it in the tiny gap between her front teeth, she gasped.

He stroked her upper arms as their tongues tangled together. When he drew away this time her mouth chased him for half a second before she scowled and thrust him away.

"You've had your first kiss."

"I have. And you didn't remain unaffected. Your microscope and all its various parts will remain in my possession."

"Next time, you shall be the one chasing after me."

# *Chapter Eleven*

H E BRUSHED HIS KNUCKLE over the tip of her nose. "It pleases me that you aren't faint of heart."

Jess drew up so she could look down the nose he'd just caressed. "I have never been afraid of you, Cadoc Morgan. Even when you act the cur." Jess finally knew the truth. She'd never been afraid of him - only of her reaction to him. When he'd kissed her, the antagonism she felt had quickly morphed into something entirely different.

He surveyed her for a moment, his expression inscrutable. "Good," he finally said. "That means you'll stop avoiding me."

"I can't afford to avoid you," she grumbled. "Not if I ever want to see my microscope again."

"Would you like to try again tomorrow evening?"

"All of my sisters will be home, including the two who are bringing their husbands in tow. I don't think I'll be able to escape."

"Then I shall retrieve you."

"Arie and Fran can be especially overprotective. And Lavinia is likely to skewer you. You owe her an apology." Arie had mothered Jess from the time she was five years of age. She'd assumed the role of both their deceased mother and their negligent father, and was like a man-eating tiger when it came to her younger sisters. Even though she now had a babe of her own and four stepdaughters. Fran tried to run everyone's lives and Vin grumbled and said it was because she kept company with Florence Nightingale. Jess suspected she was right.

"I will do everything in my power to reassure them. They may accompany you as chaperones if they don't trust my intentions. And if I am given the opportunity, I will make amends with Lavinia."

Jess sighed. "Fine. I accept your invitation. You'll need to send a conveyance for me or drive it yourself. Be prepared to endure a long inquisition."

"Watching you squirm when they ask me about our wager will be worth the pain," he said as he winked.

"The only one of them that knows about the wager is Vin, and if she values her life she won't say a word to the rest of them."

"So you've sworn her to secrecy?"

"No, it wasn't necessary. She has plenty of secrets of her own she's keeping from them. It's the threat of mutual blackmail that keeps us in accord."

"That's how Caris and I have always been. And my elder brother before he was taken from us." There was a spark of something in his gaze before he doused it with a careless grin. "I think that's why God invented siblings, to keep us from getting too arrogant about our ability to get away with mischief."

Jess wanted to tell him she was sorry for his loss. To admit that she had losses of her own and she missed the soft croon of her mother's voice at the oddest moments. To confess she'd worried over Fran every single day when her sister set off for the Crimea, especially when she heard about the conditions in Scutari. She did none of those things - because she was certain if she did he would discount them. "Then you won't be surprised by any of their questions."

He sniggered. "Raising four younger sisters inured me to surprise."

"If you raised your sisters, you and Arie will probably bond over your shared horrific experiences. She'll probably tread lightly if you lead with that."

"What about your other sisters?"

"The only one you need to really worry about is Frances. But she'll only be giving you half of her attention if her husband Mac's there. I would hope for that outcome if I were you."

"I assure you, I'm accustomed to meddling siblings. I'll be there at six o'clock," he said and held out her cloak.

His touch on her shoulders lingered for the briefest of moments, and his inhale was audible. Jess rearranged the cloak, pulling it tighter so it dislodged his hands. She silently reminded herself of her resolution to make this thing between them her own experiment. "My bonnet is out of reach because you're standing in front of it," she bristled.

He turned her around and set it on her head. Long, nimble hands covered in tiny nicks and scars tied the strings in a loopy bow before he chucked her chin. "I'll see you safely home."

"It's less than three streets over. It's no longer snowing and my ankle is nearly healed. I'll be quite alright on my own. Besides, I know that your sister took the coach. I'll not ride pillory in front of you again."

He made a tsking sound. "It would be faster, but I'll respect your wishes. I'll walk beside you and lead Bacchus."

She should refuse him or discourage him. She should make it patently obvious she didn't need him to accompany her. She didn't want to do either of those things.

The kiss had made her unsteady. And she wanted the cause of her lightheadedness to soothe away her nerves.

She frowned at her folly. "I know arguing with you is pointless."

# Chapter Twelve

WHEN CADOC HAD ESCORTED her home, he'd led his horse the entire way, their arms brushing together for a quarter of a mile. He hadn't deliberately touched her again. He'd just tipped his hat and left her at the doorstep murmuring, "Until tomorrow."

When he finally knocked on the door of the cottage, she was both relieved and at the end of her patience. She pulled him inside and said, "They're waiting for us in the parlor. I spent the entire day fending off their meddling questions about why it took me so long to get home last evening."

"Your sisters?"

She tossed a grim smile over her shoulder. "And my two brothers-in-law."

When the door to the parlor swung open, Cadoc understood her grim smile.

Two large men were lounging in the chairs nearest the fireplace with their booted heels resting on their knees and their arms crossed identically over their broad chests. They both scowled when he entered the room. The five women perched on the seat and arms of the sofa weren't scowling, but they weren't smiling either.

"Mr. Morgan, may I introduce you to my family?"

The two men stood, but the women did not.

"Jess, we don't need an introduction. We know who he is by sight and by reputation."

The woman who'd spoken held an infant in her arms and he knew immediately she was Jess's eldest sister, Araminta.

One of the men stepped forward and offered his hand. "Thaddeus St. Simon. My wife is as protective of her sisters as she is of her own brood. As am I."

Cadoc shook the man's hand. It was rough, with callouses across the palm, and enveloped his own. He set aside the urge to engage in a battle of wills and strength.

The other man extended his hand as well. When Cadoc accepted it, the lean pressure of his fingers nearly crushed Cad's. "I'm Cormac Byrne. I'm well versed in the extraction of internal organs. As is my wife."

The warning was very clear. Cad would be made to profoundly regret any harm he caused Jess Wainwright. The cost of breaking her heart would very likely be his life.

"I understand," he said as he nodded at the two of them. They nodded back to acknowledge his promise. It was a promise, Cad realized. The kiss in the cloakroom had felt like both an adventure and a homecoming. Like he'd been there before, with the honeyed scent of her skin and the dark cherry-rich taste of her lips.

He wanted to explore whatever was happening between them, but he respected Jess Wainwright's independence and fortitude too much to coax her surrender if it was against her conscience. His nod had been a promise to refrain from doing exactly that.

With all of Jess's looming, glaring family packed into the room, there was little Cadoc could do but fold his hands behind his back and remain standing.

"I must confess, Mr. Morgan, I'm not entirely persuaded that your intentions toward our sister are honorable." The eldest sister narrowed her gaze over the head of the babe she was cradling.

The babe was fussing, and Cadoc suspected it needed to burp. "When my sister was wee, the only thing that would work was moving her legs back and forth. Like she was a little soldier marching down the road."

The woman gave him an amused glance. "You are full of surprises."

"You're not here to give my wife child-rearing advice, Morgan."

St. Simon sounded aggravated, and when Cadoc turned, he was glowering.

"I know why I'm here, St. Simon. This interrogation is meant to be a show of force. To make me aware beyond the shadow of a doubt that if I trifle with Miss Wainwright's affections I'll live to regret it."

"You'd do well to remember it," the surly doctor informed him.

"Is this ridiculous charade at an end?" Jess challenged with her hands on her hips. "I am a grown woman and perfectly capable of resisting Morgan's charms. If he is too forward he'll become very well-acquainted with my knee."

Her vehemence amused him and he bowed to the room at large. "I vow to return Miss Wainwright unmolested. And at a decent hour."

"Unmolested doesn't necessarily mean unbothered. I'll know if you lay your paws on her," called her sister Lavinia as they left the room.

Jess slipped her hand into the crook of his elbow and mutely stood when he swirled her cloak around her shoulders and raised the hood.

She stopped abruptly at the sight of his surrey. "You've brought a conveyance this time instead of forcing me to ride pillory?"

"I endeavor to remain above censure."

She made a harrumphing sound as she ascended the steps. "That would be a first," he heard her mutter under her breath.

He climbed in behind her and folded himself onto the opposite seat. When he removed his hat, she looked on in alarm.

"Relax my little pragmatist. I don't have plans to ravish you. At least not in a carriage."

They rode in silence, the only sound the breaths between them. He studied her profile as she stared out the window and studiously ignored him.

Once they arrived, he escorted her down the steps. "One moment – I need to pay the hostler and send him on his way."

She raised a brow, but in a display of uncharacteristic obedience, she stood in place.

After Cadoc had paid the boy, he swept her through the front door.

He took her cloak and bonnet from her, and immediately missed the intimacy of sweeping it over her shoulders.

She folded her hands primly in front of her. "You won't get under my skin this time, Mr. Morgan. In fact, I should like a tour of the library I glimpsed when we've finished our supper."

"We don't often have company. I meet with my investors and business associates in London, not here. You shall be one of the first outside my family to view my other inner sanctum."

"Your other inner sanctum?"

He gave her a guileless smile. "My workshop and laboratory."

"Your workspace is usually a restricted area? You're the one who bade me follow you."

"My sister and the children were in the back garden, so there was no one else available to answer the door."

"Why have you not hired help? This home is one of the most substantial in the parish."

He lifted a shoulder as he pulled out her chair. "I treasure my privacy and don't want people tramping about."

"I treasure mine as well- though I seldom have the opportunity to enjoy it."

"Siblings don't often respect our need for solitude." he acknowledged. "Let me retrieve our simple fare and we'll share a meal."

He'd set the table before he left, and the soup would still be warm in the cast iron pot. He stoked the fire to life again and ladled the stew into two bowls. When he slid her bowl in front of her, she looked up from her contemplation of her ha

"So finding solitude is something you still must contend with it? Even in a home this spacious?" She continued as of the thread of conversation hadn't been severed when he left the room.

He gave her a rueful smile. "I took the responsibility of raising my four younger sisters when I was barely fourteen, and that was in a cottage much smaller than the one you share with your sisters. Although I wouldn't trade the experience, or the patience and fortitude it instilled in me, my siblings have always been underfoot. The only time Caris and my niece and nephew keep their distance is when I'm in my workshop."

She rearranged her spoon on her napkin and rested her chin in her hands. "What do you work on in your workshop, Mr. Morgan? From what I observed, there appeared to be half a dozen unfinished projects lying about."

He leaned back in his chair. "Are you truly curious or are you stalling for time, Miss Wainwright?"

Her grin was unapologetic. "A bit of both, I must confess."

"I know immediately if a design isn't going to work as I intended it to. Until I devise a way to dismantle it and refashion it into something else, I leave it in its unfinished state." Cadoc shrugged self-consciously. "I've learned it's easier for me to visualize the particular possibilities of each piece when I leave them intact."

His companion's expression turned introspective. "Hmmm, much the same way I ponder a drawing when I'm not sure which direction I plan to take."

"Your drawings of insects?"

"Primarily," she said with a nod as she swallowed a spoonful of the soup. "Although I often turn my pencil to other things as well. Especially since I haven't had the use of my microscope to more realistically render the intricacies that aren't visible to the naked eye. The suborder Anisoptera contains thousands of species, and I plan to record my findings on the fifty or so species I've encountered here in Cumbria."

As he scraped the last of his own soup from his bowl, he watched her push a wave of hair from her forehead, and marveled at her tenacity. "What sort of findings will you record?"

"Most of their membranous wings have colored markings, and the front and rear wings are shaped differently. A dragonfly rests with its wings spread horizontally and we believe some species migrate thousands of miles."

Her expression was avid and she'd been gesticulating passionately as she talked. Cadoc could care less about her dragonflies, but her passion was irresistible. "Tell me more."

"The way they catch their prey is fiendishly savage," she paused to swallow a mouthful of stew. "They have pincers like fangs, a serrated mandible, they use to catch and pin their prey, and one of my colleagues has divided them into four different classes. He calls them sprawlers, burrowers, hiders and claspers."

"What is the difference?"

She abandoned her soup to lean forward, placing her elbows on the table. "They've each adapted to a microhabitat within their freshwater environment. My favorite species is the emperor dragonfly. I've seen it consume its prey mid-air. As if it can't be bothered to take even a moment's rest."

"I assume they have relatively short lifespans. Like most insects."

"That's not quite the case. Some of the larger species may spend a year or more as larvae after they are hatched - until they shed their exoskeleton. Once the nymphs have shed the exoskeleton, it can take as little as a quarter of an hour for it to transform into a full-grown adult. As full-grown adults, their lifespan rarely exceeds eight weeks. They make the most of the time they have, though," she wistfully finished.

"How so?" He wanted to know what the root of that wistful tone was.

"Their lives are brutal, but beautiful as well. A savage dance for survival in a world that might seem small and nondescript to an outside observer."

Her wistfulness suddenly made sense. "Are you comparing yourself to a dragonfly, Jess Wainwright?"

She studied her soup, letting it drip from her spoon. "Perhaps I am." She raised her head, a fierce look in her eyes.

"What you are trying to accomplish with my niece and nephew and your other students has not escaped my notice. Indeed, it is what captivated me in the first place, my little dragonfly."

"What is it you think I am trying to accomplish, Mr. Morgan?" She asked, obviously determined to ignore his endearment.

Cad leaned forward and placed his own elbows on the table, mere inches from hers. "I think you are trying to show them there is a bigger world out there, that it is theirs for the taking. You teach for the same reasons I organize."

"The world can be very unfair to those who don't have the tools to combat its injustice. I am lucky that our sister Arie taught all of us to read - that our mother taught her. I am lucky to have been raised in a family of sisters who value inquisitiveness and independence. I want to share those values with my students. Especially the girls in my care. To show them their future needn't be constrained by marriage vows and childbearing."

Cadoc nodded. "As I said, we are motivated to achieve the same goal. Awareness that there is another path than the one the idle rich would confine us to. The working class has a capital the rich need to survive - our sweat and labor. Without them there is no industry or progress. Parliament would do well to remember it. Especially in regards to the mining community."

# Chapter Thirteen



"**Y**OUR WORK ON BEHALF of the mining community when you're here in Cumbria can't be very effective," Jess observed.

"My inventions have given miners better lighting, and eliminated the need for drammers and other child laborers like the one I once was. They've also provided me with the resources to bend the ears of politicians and journalists sympathetic to my cause, and given me leverage to insist on certain working conditions before I'll sell what I've made to anyone in the business."

"How can you be sure they don't simply revert to their former practices when you're gone?"

He grimaced at her question. "It's a risk. But to my knowledge, it's only happened on one occasion. The owner had a revolt on his hands when he tried to reinstate the previous working conditions. He quickly saw the error of his ways."

"I applaud your commitment and determination, Mr. Morgan."

"At least something I've done has earned your approval," he said with a wry smile.

Jess laid her spoon across the top of her bowl and propped her chin in her hands. "I've finished my meal, so perhaps you'll find other ways to redeem yourself. Showing me your library would be a wonderful start."

He set his own spoon down, crossed his arms and raised a brow. "My library? You mean for me to share my other inner sanctum?"

Jess fluttered her lashes at him. "Good sir, I've had multiple reports of its treasures and I am eager to see them with my own eyes."

Her dinner companion laughed. "My niece and nephew greatly exaggerate its grandeur. But, come along." He stood and pulled her chair away from the table. Jess slipped her hand through his arm with an eager smile.

When he pushed the heavy oak doors wide open, Jess clasped her hands and whirled about to take it all in.

It was a treasure trove. The gas lamps on either side of the desk and in the corners shown softly on the floor to ceiling bookshelves that lined the walls. Jess strode closer and set her hand against the wheeled ladder propped in the corner.

"May I investigate?"

"Of course. I'm gratified that something else about me has met with your approval."

"You have so many resources at your disposal, resources that would be extremely welcome in my classroom."

"I'd not deny your students access."

"I'd like a closer look at the top shelf - I spy a copy of Aristotle's De Anima."

He bowed slightly. "Be my guest. Consider my library yours whenever you need it."

Jess took her skirts in one hand and climbed to the second step from the top.

There was an entire shelf full of natural sciences translations behind her. She should be focused on them, not the width of his shoulders or the determined glint in his eyes when she turned to face him.

"You just gave me leave to use your library," she said, her voice laced with suspicion.

"Indeed I did. Do you know why, Jess?"

She gulped and gripped the rung of the ladder at her shoulders. "Because you know the lessons I design for your niece and nephew will be more thorough."

His laugh was a low rumble. "No, my little pragmatic schoolteacher. That's not why I offered you full access to my collection."

Jess could feel the heat flushing her neck and cheeks. "Then I'm sure your reasons were nefarious."

He stalked closer, until he stood mere inches from the ladder, crowding her space. His thighs brushed against the rustle of her skirts when he placed his hands on the shelves and caged her in. "I've been dreaming of doing scandalous things to you while you're perched on this ladder."

"Scandalous things?" Jess hated how breathless she sounded.

"Scandalous things," he repeated as his hand slid up her calf beneath the flannel petticoat.

"I thought we agreed to kisses."

"This is a kiss, madam," he said as he pressed his mouth to her knee.

He rubbed his knuckle against her skin and the ribbon securing her stocking. And then his lips feathered across her inner thigh.

"What are you doing?" She eked out.

"Kissing you. As we agreed. Are you brave enough to withstand it?" He asked against her thigh with a wicked smirk and eyes alight with laughter and challenge.

Jess had read of such things, but they'd seemed unimaginable. The scandalous etchings and poetry Arie shared with her sisters after her husband's death had been titillating, but she hadn't been able to visualize them until this man kissed her.

"Perhaps such kisses are a bit premature? Perhaps I'm not yet brave enough to withstand them?"

Something flickered in his gaze when he raised it to hers. If Jess hadn't been so convinced he was a reprobate at heart, she would have called it guilt.

"Then I shall indulge my curiosity in other ways - until yours is as undeniable as mine."

His fingers were on the buttons running down her back, swift and sure, before she had the chance to protest. Faster than she could blink, his deft touch was against her bare skin, sliding beneath the neckline of her dress to dip into her decolletage.

"I've dreamt of kissing you here as well," he murmured as he pressed his mouth to the flushed skin above her cleavage. "And here," he whispered against the cotton chemise stretched over the rise of her breasts. "And here," he said as he tugged her dress to her waist and began unlacing her half-corset, pressing kisses along the path of the strings.

"These kisses seem premature as well," Jess protested. She closed her eyes against the warmth of his breath on her skin. It was like the heat of the brazier against the soles of her feet on a cold night.

"They are not premature, they are an essential element of my strategy to disarm and disconcert you."

"My reaction in the coatroom was an anomaly," Jess insisted.

"Then this should not move you in the least," he said as he dipped his head to her cotton covered left breast. He curved his palm beneath it and lifted it closer, and then swirled his tongue around the tip.

Jess clenched the ladder so hard she was certain she'd have splinters as a reward. When he pulled the material tight she looked down and her nipple was like a rosebud under the nearly transparent cotton. She tilted her head back and let it rest against the ladder.

"Are you overcome with ardor, yet, dragonfly?"

"Speaking of dragonflies," Jess answered. Perhaps if she talked about her studies she could focus on something besides his wicked mouth. "Did you know their vision is a complete three hundred and sixty degrees and it's estimated they may have as many as thirty thousand lenses in their eyes?"

"Are you trying to distract me or yourself? I shan't be distracted. If you feel the need to spout random facts in the middle of my seduction, I think it's a sign you're once again in danger of losing the wager."

His lips closed over her breast once again, and he rolled the bead of her nipple against the roof of his mouth before he nipped it gently. His hand closed around the other one and tugged gently, until the abrasion of her dress against it nearly drove Jess mad. She clenched her teeth and nearly cried out when she bit her tongue as she tried to swallow a moan.

"I do not think you are unmoved, Jess Wainwright. Can you manage any more facts about your beloved insects without sounding short of breath?"

"The smallest dragonfly," she paused to regulate her breathing, "has a wingspan of a mere seven tenths of an inch."

"Go on," he said as he pulled the ribbon loose from her chemise.

"Some entomologists believe dragonflies were flying about in the time of the dinosaurs."

"That's quite a history," he murmured as he kissed her bared breast. His lips were like satin, and the suction of his mouth made her stomach tight and quivery. She wanted to tangle her fingers in his hair and squeeze her thighs together instead of remaining still as a statue.

"They've found some of them encased in ancient amber, preserved to the tiniest detail."

"I'd preserve these in amber if I could," he said as he lavished first one breast, then the other.

His tongue stroked over her areola, teasing around the place she desperately wanted to feel its caress again. She steadfastly ignored her instincts and surreptitiously curled her foot around the leg of the ladder, to stop her body from surging forward.

"That's what sculptures are for," she retorted. She wanted to bite her tongue, or turn the clock back as soon as she let the words slip.

"Are you giving me leave to sculpt your bosom, dragonfly?"

"You have plenty of women who'd willingly pose for such a scandalous endeavor. I am not among their number."

"Perhaps I'll attempt to do it from memory. With the taste and scent of you still on my tongue."

"You shall do no such thing. I forbid it."

He scraped his teeth over each nipple. "You cannot stop me. Unless you monitor my every move. Even then, you wouldn't be able to stop me from creating a memorial to these glorious beauties."

"They are simply breasts." Jess was mortified.

"They are not simply breasts. Look at how they fill my palms to overflowing." His voice grew even rougher, like the sound of a scythe separating chaff from wheat. "Look at the way your nipples harden in my palms, how they're the color of port. How they pebble at the stroke of my thumb like pert little rosebuds. How the dusky halo of your areola looks against the freckles scattered across your collarbones. They are not simply breasts. They are your breasts - just as perfectly bountiful as I imagined they would be a thousand times."

"A thousand times?"

"More than that. At least a hundred thousand times. Thinking of the way they would hold the length of my cock. If you'd be too shocked to wrap your mouth around the head and suck as I sucked these little berries to ripe, delicious fruition." He flicked his thumbs over her sensitive skin, a rough stroke that made it almost impossible to ignore his ministrations.

Every inch of her body felt alive - as if she was on the verge of shattering into a million pieces. But she couldn't let him win again.

"Your seduction ploy tonight has failed, Mr. Morgan. I have been steadfast and withstood your persuasion. Not a single whimper or moan has passed my lips."

He placed a lingering kiss on the top of each breast before he rose to his feet.

"I concede to your indomitable will, dragonfly. I will bring one of the lenses with me to Christmas dinner."

"One of the lenses? Not the entire microscope?" How much more of this was she expected to endure?

"Yes," he said as he tucked her back into her chemise and retied the ribbon. "One lens. There are three lenses and the microscope itself. For every kiss you remain impervious to, I will deliver a part. I have at least three more opportunities to storm your castle."

She pushed his hands away and loosely affixed her corset. "I welcome the skirmishes. I am confident I shall emerge victorious, just as I have tonight."

He tipped her chin up with one knuckle, his gaze roving her face. "You are a much worthier opponent than I thought you would be. I welcome the challenge, dragonfly."

She frowned. "I wish you would stop calling me that."

"You may wish all you want, madam. Futilely. I shall call you whatever I please," he said as he pulled up her sleeves. "Turn around and I'll button you back up. And you may want to fix your hair in the mirror over the mantel."

Jess wasn't a contortionist, so she ignored the warmth of his touch as he made her presentable once again. When she felt the last button slip into place at her nape, she stepped away and stood on the tips of her toes to measure the damage done to her coiffure. Her reflection showed that several of the pins had come loose. She removed them and clenched them between her teeth while she smoothed back the flyaway tendrils of hair. Once she was satisfied with her efforts, she carefully slipped the pins back in place.

"Prim and proper to the core," her host commented with what she sensed was chagrin.

"Unlike you, I have a houseful of people awaiting my return. A houseful of people you assured of my safety and well-being, might I add."

"I've compromised neither your safety nor your well-being. This is an agreement between adults, and your determination to win tonight's bout was admirable. I cede victory to you and look forward to our next engagement."

"I shall see you in two days hence."

"Not so fast, dragonfly. I will escort you home in my carriage."

<hr>

As soon as Jess closed the door behind her, Emily called out. "You've returned far earlier than we expected, little sister."

When Jess rounded the corner, her sisters were all seated at the kitchen table, their cups of tea clasped in front of them, expectant looks on their faces.

"Where are Mac and Thaddeus?" Jess asked.

"They're both on bedtime duty. We relegated them to reading Grimm's to the girls."

"Why? This feels like some sort of ambush."

"Sit down, Jess. It's not an ambush. We're simply worried about your relationship with Mr. Morgan and what his intentions are."

"My relationship with Mr. Morgan is none of your concern."

"Jess, we know that he's the first man you've ever truly shown an interest in," said Vin.

Jess flashed her a warning look. She didn't want their conversation about contraceptives and blackmail to provide even more fodder for their elder sisters.

Vin gave her an almost imperceptible nod. Letting her know her secrets were still safe.

"And he's not what we imagined for you," Emily clarified.

"I'm twenty-eight years of age and I know my own mind. While I appreciate your advice, I don't require it. I don't know how much Vin has told you, but Mr. Morgan and I have a bargain. Though it wasn't one I made fully of my own volition, I am prepared to face the consequences of my actions. Whatever they may be."

"I always thought you'd settle down with the vicar's son once he returned from Cambridge. The two of you share a scientific bent of mind and he's just as uncomfortable in social settings as you are."

Jess took a deep breath so she wouldn't say something in anger she'd be forced to regret at her leisure. When her sisters got their hackles up in her defense, as they were doing now, it felt more like intrusion than protection. She longed for Cece's stalwart support, or for an adventure of her own to finally declare her independence in a way they couldn't refute.

"Jonathan Trowbridge is a dour, gloomy mud puddle of a man. We have absolutely nothing in common. He is fascinated with igneous rock and volcanoes, and my interests lie in cataloging the insect world. He hates social functions because he thinks he's above them. I detest social functions because I often feel they are a waste of precious time filled with nothing but silly gossip."

Arie and Fran exchanged a glance and Jess wanted to skewer them. She knew what that shared amusement meant. That they found her naive. "Why don't you spend more time on these two?" She asked as she gestured toward Vin and Emily. "In case you haven't noticed, they are more firmly on the shelf than I am and show no inclination to settle down."

"Their day of reckoning will soon be at hand. They are not currently the object of my concern. You are. I will accept your assurance that I needn't worry on your behalf, but I do so with reservations. I've been putting your welfare before my own most of my life, and it's a habit I find difficult to break," Arie said.

Jess took her eldest sister's outstretched hands. "I understand. All of us appreciate the way you took care of us when mother died and father neglected us. But just as we told you when you insisted you needed to remain in your dead husband's household - we all need to seek our own happiness and make our own mistakes. I want the chance to find my own way. Just as you and Fran have and just as Cece is doing."

Her other sisters stood and each of them hugged her in turn.

"We're sorry for making you feel like a rebellious child, Jess," Fran apologized.

"And Emily and I are sorry for demanding an accountability we're not entitled to," Vin whispered into her ear as she hugged her.

Jess took a seat at the table with them after the embrace, and helped assign roles for the festivities that would begin in the morning.

# Chapter Fourteen

CADOC HAD BEEN LOATH to deposit Jess at her door because he knew he'd be returning to an empty house. It seemed even emptier with the reality of his actions looming over him like a guillotine. Every moment he spent with her forged a deeper connection. That hadn't been the purpose of their wager. At least not the one he'd admitted to himself.

George had volunteered to take Caris and the children back to Wales for the holidays, and although he was taciturn company at best, he was company. Even the housekeeper, Mrs. Hopewell, was absent. She lived in the village and helped Caris with the housework and the cooking. She was usually humming somewhere in the house from dawn until dusk. She'd informed him that morning that she wouldn't be returning until three days after Christmas.

He'd been the one to prepare the repast he'd shared with his guest, simple fare he'd mastered at the instruction of his mother. It had brought memories of her to the forefront, memories that were already there because of the holiday season. Even though they'd never had flush pockets, his Mam had always managed to make the day special. One year it was a knitted cap she'd made each of them as she sat by the fire each night. Her hands busy even after a full twelve hour day at the mines. Another year she'd managed to procure a tin of chocolate and an orange. They'd doled it out in small portions after the lamb stew she'd made.

After he rubbed down Bacchus, he let himself in the kitchen door. The house closed in around him and he suddenly ached for the sound of voices and laughter. He lit one of the kerosene lamps on the kitchen sideboard and carried it into his library. He wanted to sleep on the divan there, instead of tossing and turning in his empty bed.

Here, when he closed his eyes, the faint scent of her filled his nostrils. Like the lilies that blanketed the valley behind the family cottage. Like spring and promises and all the things he'd spent his life trying to keep safe from the greed of other men.

Despite his dastardly demands, despite the bargain he'd forced her to accept, she and her family were welcoming him to their home for Christmas dinner on the morrow. He'd never felt so conflicted and so much like the epitome of the nickname she'd called him. Cad. He was treating her like a cad. Because he was both trying to repudiate the hold she had over him and clarify his own feelings. Though she hadn't been the one to issue the invitation, she hadn't rescinded it either. Even after his manipulation of her this evening.

He couldn't help feeling a kinship with Scrooge, invited to the Cratchit family gathering in the spirit of beneficence, even though he'd done nothing to merit such an invitation.

The urge to fall asleep after frigging himself raw to the memory of the scent of spring at her nape, and the way her skin had flushed like ripe strawberries at his touch, was almost painful. But he ignored it, because after seeing her home, and with the knowledge they'd be surrounded by her family tomorrow, it felt like sacrilege.

⬦

He arrived at the Wainwright doorstep with a satchel full of oranges and chocolate. He wasn't sure of his reception and he wasn't above resorting to the bribery of those susceptible to it. Mainly the children.

When he knocked, the door was flung open by a flustered Jess. She ushered him in and two bright-eyed girls came to a staggering halt directly in front of him.

"You're Ella's uncle. Where is she?" One of them demanded in an imperious tone.

"Callie, that's enough." Jess's older sister scolded as she laid a hand on the imp's shoulder.

Cad shrugged and grinned down at the squirming child. "I don't mind. As you know, Mistress St. Simon, I am accustomed to the often unreasonable antics of children."

Thaddeus St. Simon curled an arm around his wife's shoulders. "Well met, Morgan," he said as he extended his hand in greeting.

The shake was firm this time, but not as crushing as it had been on their first meeting. Cadoc nodded. "St. Simon."

He crouched closer to the floor so he could answer the girl's question, because he didn't believe in ignoring children. Even if their parents believed the children were being impertinent. "Ella and Davy have gone to visit their cousins in Wales over the holidays."

Callie crinkled her nose. "Ella said she gets to play cricket with her brother and all her boy cousins. It's not fair. All we have in our family are girls."

"Girls can play cricket."

"Indeed they can," Emily Wainwright confirmed. "I was one of the best bowlers in my year."

"I smell oranges, Mum. I think he brought us some," a sweetly earnest voice observed.

Jess smiled. "You needn't hide behind your mother's skirts, Claire."

A diminutive little girl with cherub cheeks and fiery braids stepped away from the shelter of Jess's eldest sister and her husband. "Did you bring us oranges?" She asked as she peered up at him.

She was fairly quivering in excitement and Cadoc couldn't repress his grin. "Indeed I have brought oranges. You have a keen sense of smell, poppet."

"Papa has given us permission to play hide and seek. Might the winner have an orange as a prize?" The forthright twin's eyes were gleaming.

"I think that is a capital idea - as long as you think there are enough hiding places."

When Cadoc raised a brow in her direction, Jess shook her head in admonishment. As if she knew the mischief he was brewing.

"Dinner's ready," one of Jess's sisters called from the kitchen. Emily and the twins gamboled past them, eager to have the first pick of seating. The pace of the parents was more sedate.

"I guess I should be grateful my brother-in-law didn't give them permission to play snapdragon instead. They'd probably end up with grave injuries, or burn the house down in the process," Jess grumbled as they made their way to the parlor.

Two long tables had been shoved together, with benches as seating.

As soon as everyone had taken their place, the girls started chattering. Thaddeus gestured for silence and they turned penitent gazes toward the head of the table.

"My wife and I," he turned a worshipful gaze to Jess's eldest sister and clasped her hand, "would like to start a new holiday tradition. We'd like to go around the table and have everyone name something they are thankful for."

The impish twin bounced in her seat. "May I go first, Papa?"

Thaddeus grinned. "As if anyone could stop you when you've put your mind to something, Callie. You may proceed."

She folded her hands primly in her lap, but her eyes were shining with mischief. "I'm thankful for snow, and sleds, and warm scones, and my new mama. And for the oranges Mr. Morgan brought."

"That's more than one," said the quieter twin, Clarissa.

Callista rolled her eyes. "No one's stopping you from picking five things as well, Rissa."

Clarissa glared back. "Then I'm picking five things too. I'm thankful for fairy tales, warm socks, our new pony, my new mama and my new little sister, and," she gave her twin an arch look. "The bar of chocolate I spied in Mr. Morgan's satchel."

"Chocolate, Mr. Morgan?" Lavinia's gaze was speculative. "You've certainly upped the ante."

Cadoc cleared his throat. "You've all hospitably welcomed me into your home today. I thought it only fitting to show my appreciation. I've brought enough oranges that everyone shall have a slice, and perhaps we can enjoy the warm chocolate after the game of hide and seek I've been told is imminent."

"On that note," the physician brother-in-law spoke up. "Your Aunt Fran and I would like to remind you that rushing through your meal can cause indigestion."

The eldest child, who'd remained quiet until now, finally spoke up. "I've tried to explain how indecorous their constant interruption and rowdy behavior is."

"Clementine, thank you for striving to be an example to your younger sisters," Araminta said.

Cadoc found it amusing that she didn't praise the girl for her sentiments, but merely acknowledged the purity of her motives. Apparently, the girl's commentary struck her stepmother as sanctimonious. Cadoc's older brother Griffin had often adopted the very same attitude toward his younger siblings, and he found it gratingly familiar.

"I'd like to share what I'm thankful for," he said.

"And we'd all love to hear it," Jess sarcastically muttered under her breath.

He set his hand on her knee beneath the table and locked his gaze on her profile. "I am thankful for microscopes. And ladders. And cloakrooms. And icy roads."

Jess's muscle clenched beneath his touch as he finished his list. She stubbornly refused to look at him. Because his words rang with conviction.

"That is a very strange list, Mr. Morgan, and appears to have perturbed my sister," observed Emily. "If I were to use deductive reasoning, I'd conjecture that your list is a private joke between you."

Cadoc watched Jess's fingers tighten around her fork. "Yes. Mr. Morgan thinks to poke me up. What he doesn't realize," she lifted her head from her contemplation of her plate and scowled fiercely in his direction, "is that I grew up with six sisters and am not easily embarrassed."

"It wasn't my intention to embarrass you Miss Wain-wright."

Emily and Lavinia's gazes were flying back and forth between them with undisguised delight.

"Will you go next, little sister?" Lavinia asked.

Jess's mouth thinned and she let her hand loose itself from its death grip on her fork. "I am thankful for the opportunity to share my knowledge of the natural world with my students. I am thankful I'm sharing company with my family over the holidays."

When she seemed unwilling to offer up more, her sister Gertrude broke in. "I shall share mine."

"Nothing about me, dragonfly? Or the way I made you shatter in my library? I'm quite offended by the omission," he murmured from the side of his mouth.

"Those aren't the kind of things one expresses gratitude for when they're ensconced at the family table," she whispered back as she shifted in her seat and lifted his hand from her knee.

"Perhaps you can find another way to express your gratitude."

"You're impossible," she scoffed.

"To ignore, yes," he confidently retorted.

"Ugh."

Her exasperation made him inwardly chuckle. He planned to gain an irrefutable upper hand during the game of hide and seek.

⸺◆⸺

A half an hour after the meal had ended, when all of the adults were replete before the fire and nursing their mugs of mulled wine, St. Simon relented.

"Girls, if you'd like to play your game of hide and seek, you'll have to draw straws to determine the seeker." He'd pulled four pieces of straw from his pocket and held them in his fist.

"Does that mean the short straw is for the finder, papa?" Asked the youngest.

"Yes, Claire. Whoever draws the shortest straw must draw the other players from their hiding places."

Claire chose first, and held her piece of straw to her chest with an earnest expression. Once they'd all chosen, Thaddeus said, "Now show me what you've drawn. Flat across the palm of your hand."

All four girls obediently opened their hands.

Clementine's face darkened and Cadoc guessed she was the seeker for this round.

"I didn't even want to play," she sulked, confirming his suspicions.

"Don't be a spoilsport, Clem," chided Callista.

"Fine," she grumbled. "You lot have until I count to one hundred to secure your hiding places."

Jess whirled on her heel and headed toward the narrow staircase.

Cadoc was hot on her heels.

When she ducked into a dark wood clothes press in the corner of what appeared to be an attic, he followed.

"What are you doing?" She demanded, as she tried to push him from the wardrobe.

"Following you of course."

"This armoire won't hold the two of us."

Cadoc winked as he pulled the door closed behind him. "There aren't any shelves, dragonfly. There's plenty of room."

She pushed against his chest. "I'm not hiding in here with you. And stop calling me by that moniker."

He pressed her against the corner wall. "You'll not escape so easily. And I won't stop calling you that - it's how I think of you."

She stilled in his embrace. "You shouldn't think of me as anything besides a part of your ridiculous wager and your wards' schoolteacher."

"If only I could remain so detached," he murmured into her ear just before he nipped her earlobe.

She shifted at the sharp pain. "Biting isn't part of the wager."

"All proper kisses should involve teeth and tongue," Cadoc said as he clenched the taut muscle of her elongated neck.

Her snort was muffled. "If that is how you choose to torment me today, it will require very little effort on my part to resist your advances."

"Allow me to demonstrate my skill before you scoff at its effectiveness, Madam."

"The twins always win at hide and seek, so you don't have long. You'll have to settle for pawing at me over my clothes like one of my sister's overeager puppies."

Her attempt to dissuade him verged on the ridiculous. "I've never found it necessary to resort to pawing. Brace yourself, dragonfly. I'm determined to break through your cool facade."

The light from outside barely filtered through the crack between the door and the wall, so he couldn't make out her expression. But he felt the exasperation of her eye roll. He recognized her feigned outrage for what it was - a means of disguising her fascination. Cadoc would win this bout.

He lifted his hand to her hair and removed one of the pins that held it in place. When a heavy lock slid down the side of her neck and curled just above her cleavage, he grazed the tops of her breasts with his knuckles as he rubbed it between his thumb and forefinger.

Her sharp inhale was the only indication she was affected by his touch.

He leaned forward and slid another pin from her hair. A much larger tangle fell to her shoulders and he let it glide through his fingers like a veil. This time, there was no audible inhale, but when Cad wedged his knee firmly between hers, crushing her skirt and crinoline behind her, her breathing became winded. She didn't say a word, but her staccato little gasps filled the space between them.

He brushed the fallen coil of hair over her shoulder and bent to her ear. The moment his teeth closed gently on the tip of her earlobe, a slight tremor betrayed how much she was affected.

"It would seem you are not completely averse to teeth, dragonfly."

"You merely startled me," she huffed.

He slid his nose along her jawline, where her skin was soft with the scent of lilies.

She ground her teeth in response and he knew she was faltering. He wanted all of her iron resolve crumbled and burning at his feet. He wanted the willing surrender of her body, even if her heart and mind were still formidably opposed.

He'd take whatever morsels of hope she flung in his direction and stoke them until they became whatever he needed to convince her he was worth the risk.

"I will forge my way past all your walls, dragonfly. I'll gladly dismantle them brick by brick if that's what's required."

"I only agreed to this because you gave me no other choice."

"Although I've not been reticent regarding my desire to strip you of your garments, I didn't strip you of your choices, Miss Wainwright."

"You threatened to persecute my sister."

"Because you threatened to go to the magistrate about your purloined microscope. My threat was in retaliation."

She huffed again, slightly less indignantly. "Then do your worst, Mr. Morgan. I shall remain unmoved."

"I intend to do the exact opposite of my worst," he said as he gathered her skirts in one hand and used the other one to curl her leg around his waist. "You're going to be writhing on my thigh before we leave this wardrobe."

# Chapter Fifteen

J ESS KNEW WHAT SHE should do. And it wasn't letting him assume she was in his thrall. Emily had trained them all in self defense, but Jess had no desire to thrust her knee between his legs. She wanted to indulge in experimentation. To test her effect on him as much as he was testing his effect on her.

She shifted against his thigh and tipped her chin up. "I dare you to try, Mr. Morgan."

"You should know by now, dragonfly, that I never refuse a dare. No matter how reckless it is," he said as he hitched her more firmly against him.

When he captured her mouth, his assault was ruthless. His lips nipped at hers, demanding entry. Merciless and unforgiving of any misgivings she still harbored. She met his demands with her own. To be seen and recognized and acknowledged. In the spaces she occupied now. With no expectation of her conformity to those she wanted to cast aside and ignore.

Her lips were just as savage. She bit his bottom lip when he stroked his tongue across hers. She tangled her fingers in the unruly tousle of curl at his nape and yanked his head closer. When his tongue stroked into her mouth she quelled the feral urge to bite it in half and welcomed his exploration with one of her own.

"So this is to be a duel," he murmured into the kiss.

Jess pulled back just far enough to answer him. "Not a duel, a battle. I'm changing the terms of our wager. If I leave you panting for more, Morgan, you'll give me two lenses instead of one."

She could just make out his gleeful smile. "The dragonfly shows her claws."

"Dragonflies don't have claws, you idiot," she said.

"It was a figure of speech, madam. To let you know I welcome your little aggressions."

Her little aggressions? She'd show him exactly how minuscule her aggressions were. She lowered her hand to grapple against his waist. He was tumescent against the fall of his trousers and she grazed him there with the back of her hand. A light, teasing, purposeful touch that made him surge against her.

"I don't think we have much time until we're discovered," she said as she grazed him again.

He grunted something incoherent in response and pressed her even more forcefully against the wall at her back.

She removed the hand at her waist and set it against her breast.

"I accept your invitation," he growled and molded her against the searing warmth of his palm. She could feel it beneath the layers of her gown and her half-corset and her chemise. As keenly and sharply as she felt him swell against her own palm when she stroked his length with the delicate touch of a single, slender finger.

"It wasn't an invitation, it was a challenge. I think I can make you fall apart before you do the same to me. You're closer to the edge, blackguard."

"Blackguard? You've yet to see that side of me."

His whole body was now flush against hers, her hand crushed between them, his thumb and forefinger a ruthless caress on her breast, tweaking and tugging while they fought for dominance of the kiss.

He sipped at her lips with abandon, and he was as lost to the feel of it as she was. Jess felt as if she were drowning in the spice and heat and danger of him. She wedged her hand free and slid it beneath the hem of his shirt. When she stroked his abdomen, the rigid fortress of muscle quivered, far from invincible. She smiled slyly at the evidence of his weakness.

He was just as affected by the passion unfurling between them.

His caresses ceased and he began fumbling at her bodice, as if he was too impatient to loosen it from the back. She placed her hand in the middle of his chest and shoved.

He resisted before he let her go, with a nearly inaudible groan as his head thumped against the side of the wardrobe.

"We're done here. Your control has abandoned you and I still firmly hold the reins of my own."

His eyes glittered in the near darkness, and she could see that his lips were as plump and swollen as hers felt. As if she'd been stung. Which perhaps she had.

"Well-played, dragonfly. If you consent to visit me tomorrow, I'll surrender another lens."

They heard the thunder of feet at the same time and flung themselves into the opposite corners of their hiding places in the nick of time.

Callie and Rissa yanked open the door and shouted, "We found you!"

Cadoc threw her a hooded glance before he stepped out. "You have indeed found us," he said. "And none too soon," he muttered under his breath.

"Hullo, girls." Jess greeted them with a jaunty salute.

Rissa cocked her head. "Auntie Jess, your hair looks like you were wrestling with someone."

Jess's hand flew to her hair. It was barely pinned. She glowered at her partner in crime as he smirked. "I didn't realize I looked so ramshackle."

Callie looked her up and down with an unapologetic perusal reminiscent of her stepmother. Arie had taken Thad's girls under her wing and Jess could see her influence. "You might want to straighten your gown and fix your hair before our mother sees you."

"She insists on making us change or take a bath when we look as rumpled as you," Rissa said.

"I'll assist you in your bath," Cadoc's offer was too low for the girls to hear.

"What did you say about a bath, Mr. Morgan?"

Of course her nieces were possessed of excellent hearing. And were probably expert eavesdroppers. Jess turned to the man just beyond her shoulder. "Yes, do tell all of us what you said about a bath, Mr. Morgan," she said as she crossed her arms.

"I said wrath, not bath. I was agreeing that it might not be advisable to incur the wrath of your stepmother." His recovery was swift and the smirk he leveled in Jess's direction as he offered an explanation to her nieces was infuriating.

"Well, your room is here, so you should go make yourself presentable, Aunt Jess," said Callie.

"I'll do that before I meet you downstairs for our gift exchange."

Rissa came to a staggering halt and grabbed her sister's arm to remain upright. "We get presents besides the ones we received in our stockings this morning?"

Jess nodded. "I know there are some packages for you under the tree. And you already know that Mr. Morgan was kind enough to bring oranges for us to enjoy."

"Don't forget the chocolate," he muttered as the girls scampered away.

"I'm not," she said with a devilish grin. "I've decided the chocolate is your present for the adults to enjoy."

"If you'd like me to give you something to enjoy…"

"You're incorrigible. Go downstairs and try to win the approval of my family."

He sketched a bow. "By the time you return, I'll have them eating from the palm of my hand."

"It isn't a bear taming, Mr. Morgan."

"The size of your two brothers-in-law would suggest otherwise."

"Though you may not have their formidable height, Mr.Morgan, I'm confident you can hold your own," Jess said as she swept him a curtsy in return.

She felt his gaze on her as she walked away. Likely on her rump because he was a rogue of the first degree.

Jess's reflection in the tiny mirror above her washstand filled her with dismay. It was no wonder her nieces had pointed out her dishabille. She looked thoroughly ravaged. Thank goodness they hadn't the discernment to comment on her beestung lips and flushed collarbones.

Despite the havoc the armoire interlude had wrought with her appearance, Jess was pleased with its outcome. Cadoc Morgan might boast about his ability to make her family eat from the palm of his hand, but she knew beyond the shadow of a doubt she'd had him eating out of hers. She was the indisputable champion of their latest bout.

The key to turning Mr. Morgan's world upside down was meeting him with a fierceness of one's own. As she smoothed and repinned her hair, Jess contemplated what her discovery meant for their future interactions.

If she was able to keep him as imbalanced as she had today, she would have her microscope back in her possession before the holidays ended.

Once she was satisfied that everything was put back to rights and her sisters would suspect nothing was amiss, she made her way down to the parlor.

Vin raised a brow at her delayed entry, but didn't comment. It would have been impossible to hear her over the hubbub of the children. They each had a small stack of packages in front of them that they were ripping open one by one. They looked like wild creatures.

Cadoc had joined Thaddeus and Cormac on the floor and all three were romping around offering to be destriers. The girls were screeching with laughter as they threw ribbons and paper at them, and the men were snorting as if they were trying to dodge the ammunition exuberantly flung in their direction.

Her thief was doing his damnedest to win over her family. Jess had only been half serious when she suggested he do so- because their close association was ephemeral and she doubted it would become one of long standing.

When she took a seat on the sofa, he glanced up from his place on the floor. His irrepressible grin hit her squarely in the chest because it was carefree and brimming with boyish charm. From the little he had told her of his life, she doubted he'd had many chances for romps such as this.

His willingness to play hobby horse was obviously ingratiating him to Jess's family, and she shuddered at the mere thought of the conversation that would be demanded when he left their company.

Once Jess took a seat beside her, Arie wasted no time. "Your Mr. Morgan appears to know his way around a nursery."

*Well, that hadn't taken long.* Though Jess knew Arie's intentions were kind, they needled. Arie had always been something of a brooding hen - and now Jess felt like she was the object of all that clucking.

"Yes, he's quite accustomed to taking charge of a situation. Whether or not he's qualified to do so."

"He confided that he raised his siblings. Thad is probably the only one of us with more experience."

"He's not a marriage prospect, Arie. As much as you want him to be."

Jess's sister sighed at her harsh tone. "I didn't say he was, Jess. I was simply making an observation."

"An unwelcome and inappropriate observation. Leave it alone."

"Fine. I'll just leave you with this -" Arie paused dramatically. "The air in the room simmers between you and I've never seen you look at someone that way."

"The way I look at him is no different than the way I look at one of my preening male dragonflies."

Arie harrumphed. "If you say so."

As if he sensed he was the topic of their conversation, Cadoc lumbered to his feet and made his way over to her chair. "Miss Wainwright, the hour grows late and I have much to do in my workshop. I will take my leave of you."

Jess rose to her feet. "I'll walk you to the door."

As soon as they were out of earshot, she grabbed his forearm. "Where is the lens you promised you would deliver?"

His hand went to his pocket and she saw the flash of one of the concave mirrors before he closed his fist. "Here."

Jess's hand flailed to reach it, but he easily held it out of reach.

"You owe it to me," she bristled. "Those were the terms."

"I'll give it to you if you grant me a Christmas boon."

She braced her hands on her hips. "I think I've granted you enough favors for one day."

His arm slid around her waist and pulled her into him, before she had a chance to protest. The touch of his lips was fleeting, but the close darkness of the closet came rushing back to her, and she was on the verge of looping her arms around his neck when he stepped away. He pointed at the mistletoe hanging from the archway above their heads. His thumb scraped over her bottom lip as he grinned. "Thank you for my favor."

He eased her hand into his own and closed it around the lens.

He tipped his hat in her direction once he was bundled against the cold. Jess gave him a sharp nod in return that made him grin before the door shut behind him. Once he'd vacated her space, the shadows seemed longer and the chill in the air felt more pronounced. Jess rubbed her elbows to dispel her melancholia.

It didn't work. She needed more distraction and something to subdue the riot of her thoughts and the herd of reindeer galloping through her stomach. When she'd taken control in the wardrobe everything had slowed to the speed of molasses. Perhaps if she demanded he finish what they'd begun in the library, she could finally have a restful night.

Jess decided she'd pay a visit to Cadoc Morgan once the rest of the house was snug in their beds.

# Chapter Sixteen

T HE DAY HAD NOT been what Cadoc had expected. Jess's family disguised their hostility with the barest veneer of civility, and everyone but the children had been guarded and wary. His dragonfly hadn't allowed their disapproval to deter her, and her quiet belligerence had made him proud. Their foray in the closet had been unexpected too. Especially the way she'd ferociously returned his kiss - with a ruthless precision that made him want to keep her there, all to himself, for days. He'd been determined to make her come undone and she'd turned the tables on him. It was becoming more and more difficult to dismiss the effect she had on him because every interaction deepened his fascination instead of subduing it.

Once he'd rubbed down Bacchus, he found himself in his shop. The lighting mechanism he was working on for his new lamp design wasn't coming together, and his fingers were clumsy. Even when he pulled it nearer and bent over it with his glasses perched on the end of his nose, his touch fumbled.

He felt like a coiled spring, and knew if he didn't release all the energy that had crackled to life in her presence, the lamp would never be finished.

Since Carys and the children had gone to visit family and friends, and wouldn't be exchanging gifts of any sort, they were due back the next evening. It was the last night he'd be able to savor the solitude of a quiet house. He stripped off everything but his trousers and laced up his gloves. He pounded the sack of grain suspended from the ceiling with all his might. Like it was the source of all the ill and pestilence in the world.

It felt good to limber his muscles and dance on the balls of his feet as he cut and jabbed at his imaginary foe. He was bracing his hands on his knees when someone cleared their throat at the edge of the room.

He remembered he hadn't locked the door and shot up, his fists clenched and ready for battle.

The woman he'd taken his leave of, not an hour before, was standing at the threshold, twisting her hands in front of her.

"I thought we agreed you would retrieve the other lens tomorrow night," he said, his chest heaving.

He felt the sweat drip from his chin and splash his chest, and absently rubbed the space between his pectoral muscles. His guest's eyes darted there, and even with the distance between them, he could see she was biting her lip.

She gave herself a little shake and raised her eyes to his face. "I'm not here for the lens. I'm here because I think we should talk about what happened in the closet today and what I think it means."

"I thought it was clear what it meant. It's all part of the wager."

She remained silent.

He plucked a towel from the table and swiped it over his chest and behind his neck. "Isn't it part of the wager, dragonfly?"

"I told you, I want to change the terms of the wager. I won today. And I think my victory deserves more than the return of my lens."

He prowled closer, so close her breath feathered over his bare skin. When he raised his arm and planted his palm on the plaster just behind her head, her eyes widened in alarm.

"Did you jeopardize your safety to corner me in my home again, Miss Wainwright?"

Cad knew she and her sisters had neither horse nor carriage.

She shrugged and her shoulder grazed his forearm. "I decided to take the evening air. It seemed convenient to kill two birds with one stone."

"You walked here," he flatly said. He was furious at her rash disregard for her own well-being. He couldn't fathom that she'd been reckless enough to brave the winter cold when he'd saved her from freezing to death in the streets a fortnight ago.

She thrust up her pointed little chin. "Of course I walked here. How else was I to convey myself?"

"If this conversation was so imperative it was weighing on your mind, you could have sent word. My carriage could have picked you up."

She vigorously shook her head. "No. I didn't want to draw unnecessary attention or give my sisters reason for additional chastisement."

"So you snuck out under false pretenses."

Her cheeks flushed. "I didn't feel like listening to a lecture on the impropriety of my actions."

"As you continuously remind me, you're a grown woman. The propriety of your actions are yours and yours alone to judge. Just like the consequences of them."

"I know that. But trust me, a clandestine visit is much preferred to the bothersome headache I'd be subjected to if I sought their stamp of approval first."

"Then tell me what you're demanding from me." He needed to hear her say it. That his irrational fury wasn't unfounded. That she wanted more than his kiss.

She peered down at her hands. They were tangled together so tightly, her knuckles were stark white and the veins in her bared wrists shone lilac and translucent. "I want you to finish what you began in the library," she said, her chin tilted defiantly in his direction.

All of her singular attention was now on him, and the same coiled energy he'd sought escape from earlier rose in the space between them. "I left nothing unfinished in my library."

"When I was on the la– ladder," she stammered. "I thought you were going to touch me there."

"There?" He was deliberately obtuse.

She arrowed her finger toward her cunny, her face ruddier than a sunset.

He dropped his hand to her waist and when he splayed it across her stomach, his thumb just brushed the top of her mound over her skirt. "Here?" He asked teasingly, and swiped the fabric just below her navel.

She gulped and Cad thought it was the most adorable thing he'd ever seen. "Answer me, dragonfly. Here?"

She gave him a nearly imperceptible nod as she clenched her hands in the folds of her skirt.

"How specific is your want? If I touch you there right now, will that do? Or do you want me to touch you there while you're perched on my ladder?"

"The ladder," she confirmed and tried to duck under his arm.

If she was asking him to follow through on his original intentions, he wasn't going to let her hide behind her inhibitions. He lashed his arm around her waist. "No. You were brave a moment ago. I'll let you lead the way."

She set her chin at that ridiculously haughty angle again and he steeled himself.

"If I let you touch me there, it doesn't count. It's not part of the wager."

"It's a sort of kiss, and we agreed kisses were essential to our bargain."

"I want to know what it feels like, just once, to quiet my thoughts and simply enjoy what's happening to my body. You cornered me into this and it's the least you owe me."

He barked out a laugh. "Now?"

She lifted a shoulder as if to say what better time, then now?

He shrugged in response and flashed a quick grin. "Follow me."

She didn't resist when he tangled their fingers together and tugged her alongside him. Her lack of resistance pleased him more than anything had in a very long time.

"I want to peruse your library at my leisure."

"Before or after the ladder, dragonfly?"

"After. And I remember how to get there on my own, Mr. Morgan. Your house isn't that big," she grumbled.

"Still, I can't risk you becoming lost and delaying our mutual pleasure."

Cadoc had the irrepressible urge to twist her remark into some filthy innuendo. To remind her of the way she'd soon be keening beneath his mouth as her body shuddered against the ladder. He wanted to remind her she'd soon be caging his head between her knees and fisting her hands in his hair. He withstood it, because he couldn't bear chasing her away.

He wryly acknowledged he was already lending credence to Carys's observation that his attachment bordered on obsession.

When he pushed open the door, her sigh echoed across the empty threshold. "I can smell the pages," she murmured.

Cadoc's collection included tomes he'd found at bookseller stalls, and though the worn leather bindings lent a certain ambience, he found them musty. He'd only purchased the books because many of them were obscure treatises on engineering that were now out of print.

"I don't know many people who would share your fascination. Usually, it induces sneezing, not sighing."

She shot him a smile over her shoulder. "It's well-ventilated and quiet. And there's enough material here to occupy my mind for years."

When they reached the far corner of the room, she hesitated. The ladder rose in front of them as if it was imbued with its own sentience.

"Are you going to climb it?" He whispered into the curve of her neck. The urge to coax her into submission was insatiable. He tamped it down.

"Yes, but I need you to distract me."

He cupped her from behind and scraped his teeth along her throat. "Up you go, dragonfly."

She leaned forward on a gasp and climbed to the second rung.

"Now, raise your skirts for me."

Cadoc wanted to see the perfect peach of her arse, to flex his hands over it as he devoured her. She inched up her skirt and petticoat as he dropped to his knees.

"Don't you want me to turn around?"

He chuckled at her confusion. "No, I want to stroke your little pearl just like this."

Her mound was bare, and he brushed aside the fabric covering her thighs so he could smell and taste her.

She rose to the tips of her toes and moaned when he nipped her inner thigh. A trickle of her juices slicked the skin, and he lapped it up with a groan as he clutched her to him. "Your little hotbox is wet and ready, dragonfly."

She shifted back, thrusting her body more fully in his grasp.

"Stop preening and apply yourself," she grumbled.

"You're very demanding for someone who's asked a favor of me."

"You have only yourself to blame for that conundrum."

# *Chapter Seventeen*

J ESS HAD ONLY SEEN one illustration of what he was preparing to do to her. In that picture, the courtesan had sprawled with abandon over a coverlet while a man buried his face between her legs. The woman's back had been arched, and her hands were tangled in her lover's hair.

In her naivete, Jess had thought that was the only way to position herself.

When his teeth grazed her inner thigh again, she set her nerves aside. She knew she was woefully ignorant of all but the most straightforward lovemaking. "Although this isn't quite what I pictured, I'm placing myself in your hands," she informed him somewhat primly.

He laughed into her skin, and the rumble of it made her body clench. "This isn't a lesson, Jess. Let your body relax and enjoy the experience."

Jess took a deep breath and willed her muscles to surrender to what he was doing.

"Good girl," he murmured, as he skated his nose up her thigh again.

"I'm not your girl," she groused as her body tingled. "Good or otherwise."

"In this moment, right here, right now, that's exactly what you are," he contradicted as he nipped her skin. And then his mouth was right there, swallowing the bundle of nerves. She bucked against him and he laughed again. His tongue swirled over her and she could feel herself quaking and melting. She'd been on edge for days, worried about her sisters' protective gestures and what the repercussions of this agreement would be, and  this felt like a reconciliation of what she wanted but was afraid to claim.

She glanced over her shoulder and the sight of him clearly enjoying her torment, his eyes closed in concentration, made everything inside her start to climb. "This isn't part of our wager, we agreed," she reminded him again.

"Just let go, dragonfly. And stop talking," he reprimanded with a slap to her bared cheeks. She gasped at the sting, and the determined suction of his tongue. She was gripping the ladder so hard she was afraid she'd have splinters.

She held her skirts in one hand and watched as he licked two of his fingers. When he thrust them inside her and bit down subtly on her clitoris she rose to her toes. She was desperate to escape the pressure, but she never wanted it to end.

Her hips ground against his face and he groaned. That naughty, feral groan was what her body had been waiting for. The pulse started in her sternum and lodged in her stomach, and then in her center.

Jess finally let go. He swallowed all of it as her legs shook and she sagged against the ladder. He had an iron grip on her hip, holding her there while he gulped down her release. If he'd possessed the temerity to loosen it, she'd have sunk to the floor. Boneless and dazed.

When he stroked her back and set the hand that had been holding her skirts firmly on the ladder again, she was suddenly shy.

He rose to his feet, and when he tipped her face toward him, she could see the glistening drops of her arousal in his beard. "You've no reason to be ashamed. Especially not with me." He brushed a soaked lock of hair from her neck.

"It was over quickly - and you received nothing in return."

He kissed her then, and she could taste herself on his tongue. "I wanted to see you come apart for me, dragonfly." He lifted her hand and pressed it to the front of his trousers. They were wet and the grin he tossed her was smug. "I received what I wanted in return. I'll receive it again when I remember how you looked when you finally let me give you what you needed."

"That's all it took for you to spend as well?" She asked in astonishment.

"Only with you. It was a near thing in the wardrobe today. The alchemy you wield is a dangerous thing to my self-control."

Now Jess was the one who felt like preening. She considered her mission an unmitigated success. She'd wanted to assert a sort of dominance over him, because she'd loved the feel of the power sluicing through her veins in the wardrobe.

"I like the thought of my alchemy rendering you senseless and chaotic."

His chuckle held a bitter edge. "More fool I for letting you find the chinks in my armor," he said as he took her hand and pulled her toward the settee in the center of the room. He collapsed onto it, and dragged her onto his lap.

She resisted at first, wrapping her hands around his biceps and straining away. He grinned and shook his head.

"The hour grows late and I need to avoid discovery."

"A quarter of an hour more will arouse no suspicions."

"Only for a moment." Jess was relenting because she'd never in her life felt so untethered and without a compass.

He settled his hands around her waist and she leaned in, until her head was nestled in the crook between his shoulder and neck. She pressed her face to the skin there and inhaled the scent of sulfur and leather that always seemed to cling to him.

"Tell me about the mines," she murmured.

His chest rose and fell in a deep sigh, and she sensed his reluctance.

"I try not to think about the mines and all they took from me."

"You've revealed virtually nothing about whence you came and why you settled in Heathsted."

He tipped his head and rested it against the tufted back of the sofa. "Caris and I settled here because our sister Gwyn wed a man from hereabouts. Simon Cuthbert. When he got the gold bug, she followed him to California, and left Davy and Ella in our keeping."

"Why would she leave her children behind?"

"They didn't know what awaited them in America, and she promised to send for them once they were settled. Her letters have become more and more infrequent, and the most recent one..." He blew out another sigh and closed his eyes.

"The most recent one?" Jess prompted.

"She finally told us she'd decided to leave Davy and Ella here - and asked if I'd become their permanent guardian."

"You seem conflicted about her decision."

His eyes flickered open and his gaze centered on hers. "I understand her reasons, and I love them. I'm not hesitating because of that. My sisters and I lost our father when we were too young to remember him, and our mother and our eldest brother to a mine explosion when I was barely fourteen. To willingly give up the keeping of those dearest to you? I cannot fathom it."

In that moment Jess finally acknowledged to herself that Cadoc Morgan was far more complex and intriguing than she'd first thought. "That's why you stepped in to raise your sisters? Even though you were nearly as young?"

His expression closed. "There was no one else to do it. I did what I had to because Ma wouldn't have wanted us separated. And my elder brother Griffin would have found a way to haunt me to the end of my days."

She laid her head against his chest. "I was barely five when our mother died. Arie is truly the only mother I've ever known. Our father fell apart after the funeral, and it was up to her to keep us in shoes and food. Even after he roused himself from the pit of drunkenness, he sought comfort elsewhere. We recently found out we have a gaggle of half sisters we knew nothing of."

"My old man loved the bottle far too much as well. To the detriment of everything else in his life. Including his family. I think Mam was relieved when one of the dray carts mowed him down as he was stumbling home."

"And what of your brother Griffin? Do you think he was relieved?"

"I think he was relieved, but sorry too. Da was the one who taught all of us to sing. And he used to write all of the things he used to compete in the Eisteddfod."

"What is the Eisteddfod?" The word mangled itself on her tongue.

"It's a Welsh singing competition. Before he passed, Da placed in it almost every year. Griff followed in his footsteps and he nearly won everything the year before he died."

"So all of you can sing?"

"We can all carry a tune, but Griff was the one who inherited Da's bardish talents."

"Will you sing something for me?"

He began with a low hum, and then she felt the rumble of the words building beneath the ear pressed against his chest. His warm baritone surrounded her, like hot tea and a shawl.

*"When thy father went a-hunting, a spear on his shoulder, a club in his hand. He would call the nimble hounds, 'Giff, Gaff; catch, catch, fetch, fetch!' He would kill a fish in his coracle as a lion kills its prey. When thy father went to the mountain, he would bring back a roe-buck, a wild boar, a stag, a speckled grouse from the mountain, a fish from Rhaeadr Derwennydd. Of all those that thy father reached with his lance, wild boar and lynx and fox, none escaped which was not winged."*

When his voice tapered off she remained where she was. His arms tightened around her instead of loosening - the only indication he was as loath to sever their connection as she was.

"Was that song about hunting?" She finally broke the silence to ask.

"Aye, Griffin used to sing it to all of us by the fire at night. After Da passed. It's the oldest song in our language - but I'm not as fluent as my brother was. Hence my English translation. It's a lullaby about the death of a boy's father and his legacy."

"You can hear the yearning in the melody. It's beautiful." She was too shy to tell him she thought the singing itself was beautiful, that she thought he was beautiful in ways she never expected him to be. He was a study in contrasts and the more time they spent together the more aware she became of how deep those contrasts went.

"The yearning is probably why we loved it so much. Our Da was troubled and we didn't have many good memories. We probably wanted to gild them."

"Is that why you're so overwhelming sometimes? Because you are so accustomed to fighting for everything?"

He chuckled darkly and rested his chin atop the crown of her head. "Caris says I've always been a scrapper. She said even when I was a drammer, I wrapped a cache of rocks in a rag so I'd have something to defend myself against the whip."

Jess was shocked. "They whipped you? I knew the treatment of children in the mines was deplorable, but I hadn't realized it was so bad."

"I have the scars on my back and my mangled fingers and a bum knee to prove it. But suffice to say it wasn't just the pit boss I had to watch out for. It was competitive, and there were explosions and the dust and damp all the time. I was heartily relieved twenty years ago when women and children were prohibited from going underground."

Jess nodded.  "The Mines Act of 1842. I was only eight, but when Arie read about it to us  I remember thinking I'd never again take the clean air of the countryside for granted."

She couldn't resist nuzzling into the space beneath his chin and pressing a kiss to his scruffy jawline. "Do you miss any of it now that you're standing on the outside looking in?"

She felt him swallow. "Just Griffin and Mam. I wonder if they'd be proud of what I've accomplished."

"How could they not be?" She asked as she laid her hand against his heart, and felt it thud beneath her palm and the soft lawn of his shirt.  "You're an exceptional man, Cadoc Morgan."

Jess placed a chaste kiss on his bared collarbone.

"I'm not, dragonfly. I just do as I need to."

"So you still plan on surrendering the lens I won earlier today?"

"Aye, I'll give you a moment to tidy up while I fetch it."

He rose to his feet and raised her to her own. His eyes darkened when their most intimate parts slid together, and he clenched his jaw immediately afterward.

In the beginning, Jess thought the power dynamic of their bargain was skewed in his favor. But now she was coming to know the truth. The truth was that Cadoc Morgan was more bluster and braggadocio than anything, and his defenses were the furthest thing from an impenetrable fortress imaginable. The truth was that he had made this bargain for reasons he kept to himself and sometimes the way he looked at her made Jess feel like a Greek statue on a pedestal. As if he thought she was rare and he'd be her supplicant if she asked.

He was making her question everything she thought she knew and wanted and she desperately needed to shore up her defenses against him.

# Chapter Eighteen

CADOC HADN'T WANTED TO set her away from him. He would've gladly stayed there with her curled up in his lap until they were old and gray. Her soft sighs as she'd nestled against him, the sweet, precious recline of her body curled into his. Holding her felt like the sunlight he'd basked in as a boy after the cramped darkness of the mines. But he owed her the lens.

He didn't know what he was expected to do if she won the wager and he was compelled to return her microscope in its entirety. The reality of her, with all her thorns that disguised her softness, was almost too much to bear. Perhaps letting her dismantle his armor was penitence for the duress he'd placed her under.

He thought the wager would be a way to cleanse her from his thoughts - like an exorcism. Instead, it had been a confirmation.

When he reached his workshop, he slipped the lens into his pocket and took a moment to center himself and his thoughts. It was in his nature to be playful and teasing, but that tendency became exacerbated around her and he wanted to turn everything upside down with a dare so he could see the sparkle of her eyes when she defied him.

He used a handkerchief on one of the tables to wipe the cum from his now partially flaccid cock. He was never completely unaffected around her, but at least he was no longer at full mast. Cadoc debated changing his trousers, but decided he'd relish her discomfort at being pressed against him on the ride home. Just in case she was determined to ignore what had just happened, it would be a lewd, inescapable reminder.

The sight of her on her tiptoes, a book in her hand, greeted him when he returned to the library.

"What have you found?" He asked.

She turned about with the book clasped against her chest. "You have books on farming as well as books on engineering. I want to include a discussion in my article about the relationship of dragonflies to the ecosystem, including their benefits to crop production. May I borrow this?"

"You may. My library is at your disposal, Jess. Even after our bargain ends."

Her teeth sank into her bottom lip. "So you won't turn me away once our wager has come to an end?"

"I won't. I don't think I could forget it enough to turn you away. I think there would always be a hope you were here for kisses as well as books."

She rolled her eyes at that. "You're incorrigible, Cadoc Morgan. It's nothing short of miraculous that my reputation has remained unsullied."

"Don't wreck my dreams, dragonfly," he said with a wry grin as he handed her the lens.

She gave him an inscrutable look as she slipped it into the pocket of her skirt and he envisioned the gears turning ferociously behind her hazel eyes.

He lifted her cloak from the back of his chair and held it out for her. "Let's get you home."

"If you drive your carriage through the center of town at this late hour, the gossip will be insatiable."

"We're not driving. You'll have to make do with riding in front of me on Bacchus. And we'll go through the fields so no one sees us."

She slipped under her cloak and remained still while he tied the closure at her throat and pulled the hood over her head. When he'd finished, she gave him a stern look. "No shenanigans. I've put myself to rights and I don't want questions if one of my sisters has snuck down to the kitchens for late night sustenance."

Cadoc chucked her under the chin. "I promise to keep my roving hands to myself unless absolutely necessary."

He donned his greatcoat and the red scarf Caris had left behind as his Yuletide gift. When he'd buttoned up, he winged his elbow toward her.

This time, when he lifted her onto the saddle, he let his hands linger around her waist for the merest second. Her ankle was fully healed, so she didn't cling to him. Instead she gave him a terse nod and arranged her skirts.

He smiled to himself when he swung up behind her and she held her body rigidly away from him. His arms looped around her waist and she had no choice but to relax into them. "What are you afraid of, dragonfly? I already promised to keep my hands to myself."

She sniffed. "I'm not taking any chances."

"I think you're more afraid of yourself than you are of me," he whispered roughly in her ear. "But I'll pander to your fears for now."

She sniffed again, but didn't move or reply. Her hands were wrapped around the pommel as if her life depended on it. He shook his head at her obstinacy.

There was a full moon, and the fields they crossed were barren, the shorn crops ghostly in the silvery light. A rising wind battered them from the sea to the west, and Cadoc burrowed his nose into the scarf he'd thrown about his neck. Jess shivered and he lashed her closer to the heat of his body. "There's no reason for you to become an ice block, dragonfly."

"I'm not cold," she said through chattering teeth.

"Whoa," Cadoc murmured as he tugged the reins. Bacchus came to a prancing stop and he unwound the scarf from his neck. He wrapped it around her shoulders, neck and lower face, until she was protected from the wind.

"What about you?"

"You forget, I'm accustomed to harsh working conditions. If you're worried about me, you can return it when I deposit you on your doorstep."

She pulled the scarf higher, until her entire face was hidden, and the only discernible feature left uncovered was the flutter of her lashes against her cheeks.

He unbuttoned his coat and reeled her closer, enclosing the sides of it around her as well. She didn't protest. He noted her body no longer quaked and her teeth no longer rattled her jaw.

They rode the remaining mile and a half in silence, and he was reluctant to let her go when they came to a stop at her kitchen door.

He dismounted first, and carefully lifted her into his arms. He held her there, suspended and hovering, and she didn't protest. Her unwavering, jewel-like gaze met his and he didn't feel the cold slowly seeping through his open coat. When he lowered her, she was still intoxicatingly close, her chin tipped toward him and her hands clasping his upper arms.

"I'll bid you farewell."

She nodded uncertainly, and her grasp on him remained firm. "I apologize for my uncharitable behavior. I appreciate you seeing me home."

"I could do no less. I don't know what possessed you to set off on your own, but I wasn't going to let you repeat your daft behavior."

She narrowed her eyes. "Just when I think I can tolerate you, you insult me."

He lifted her chin and dropped his head. "'Twasn't an insult, dragonfly. Merely an observation," he said against her lips. His kiss was gentle at first, so gentle she barely felt it. He deepened it, his teeth nipping at her bottom lip, coaxing her to allow him entry.

# *Chapter Nineteen*

J ESS WANTED TO STOMP on his foot or bite his lip, but when she opened her mouth beneath his, the kiss filled her stomach with a thousand wings and made her want to twirl around in a circle until she was dizzy from it. His hands slid under her cloak and fell to her hips, lifting her against him. She lifted one of her mittened hands and held it up. She didn't even need to tell him what she wanted. He removed it with his teeth and tossed it to the ground.

Jess slid her now bare hand to the back of his neck and cupped the curve of muscle notched just above his spine. He groaned and pressed her even closer, so she could feel how hard he was. The fabric that had been damp from his earlier release had dried, but was still dark.

He tilted his head away from her and growled. "If you aren't in that door in five seconds, I'll take you right here beneath the cold moonlight. Consequences be damned."

Jess took two steps back and stood there, unable to look away. She could see the puff of their breaths in the open air, feel the weight of the desire in his tortured gaze. "Flee, dragonfly. This is the last warning you'll get before I pounce."

Jess took her skirts in her hands and scurried to the door. She gave him one last look over her shoulder. He looked like some fae prince in the pale light, and she almost ran back. She pushed open the door, and quickly shut it behind her. Before she changed her mind.

When Jess descended the stairs the next morning, she was still rubbing sleep from her eyes. Her excursion and its aftermath had made her toss and turn all night, uncertain of her path and dreading its outcome.

Vin and Cece were seated at the kitchen table.

Jess skidded to a halt. "I thought you were wed now? What are you doing here?"

"She's left her husband to fend for himself," Vin clarified.

"I came on the train yesterday. It was delayed and I knew everyone would be abed, so I stayed in the room above the tavern."

Cece looked careworn and exhausted. And heartbroken. "We're glad you're here because we've missed you, but I'm heartily sorry trouble has brought you home."

Jess wanted to besiege her for advice, but sensed she carried burdens of her own.

"Your new husband has already broken faith?" Jess asked.

Cece twisted the claddagh ring over her knuckle. "I've never felt so betrayed or manipulated," she quietly confessed.

"It seems to be quite the whirlwind romance."

Jess erred on the side of tact and didn't mention any of the heated discussions Cece's sudden choice had caused. Emily had been on the verge of retrieving her from what she'd deemed an irrational lapse in judgment.

"It felt as if I knew him from the moment we met. The reason for my familiarity became quite clear."

Her sister sounded bitter, and more wracked by despair than she'd ever seen her.

"What caused the rift between you?"

Cece's bark of laughter was harsh. "His deception feels unforgivable. It was him, not Henry, who wrote the letters. His deceit made me question whether I ever held my husband's heart."

Jess and Vin both gasped in outrage.

"You told me those letters were how you came to truly know your husband," said Jess.

"And you weren't the only one swooning over his words. We all did when you read one of them aloud," added Vin.

"My husband wasn't the one you were swooning over or I was acquainting myself with. It was a big, gruff Scot like a great, wounded bear."

Jess noted that even as her sister complained, her throat was hoarse with tears and her words held grudging affection. "So you're still hopeful?"

Cece tipped her head back. "I shouldn't be. Loving Malcolm Lockhart is exasperating."

"So you really love him," Vin mused.

"He made it impossible not to," Cece grumbled. "He's caring and protective beneath all his brooding, and he truly meant the words he wrote."

"So this gulf isn't entirely irreconcilable?" Asked Jess.

"No. I fully expect him to chase after me, even though I explicitly instructed him not to."

"He'll have a whole host of your family to contend with," warned Vin. "Especially Thad and Mac. They won't let him off easily."

Cece dropped her head in her hands. "They'll probably thrash him to within an inch of his life."

"Wasn't he a soldier? He can probably hold his own."

"Yes, Vin, he was a soldier. But he also probably thinks he deserves a thrashing. Because he blames himself for everything- no matter how ridiculous it is. I'm angry at the way he deceived me, because I wasted so many years questioning what I was to Henry. Those letters were what made me doubt how well I truly knew my first husband, and the emotion poured into the pages was Mal's, not his. That's the deception I couldn't countenance on my own. All that time wasted."

"If you say he can hold his own, we'll believe you. Perhaps he can appease them with whisky. They're partial to it."

"That's something he wouldn't know he needed to bring. They'll have to share theirs."

"Are you worried for him?" Jess asked.

Cece smiled, and her whole face was full of brilliant light that Jess was envious of and wanted for herself. "I think he'll be able to hold his own, despite the fierce need of Thad and Mac to guard me against further hurt. He's used to fighting for what he wants, even if he thinks he doesn't deserve it, and I know he wants our marriage and what we've begun to build."

Jess and Vin both stretched their hands across the table and Cece grasped them.

"We're happy for you, Little Sister," Vin said and Jess nodded in agreement even as she blinked away her sudden tears.

Jess was happy for her little sister, who'd borne so much and been trapped in her own sorrow and widow's weeds for so long Jess had feared she'd be cloaked in them forever.

The way Cece had embraced the change in her life, her courage and her resilience, stalled the breath in Jess's lungs and made her chest hurt.

"Yes, we're happy for you," Jess echoed Vin's sentiment.

Cece drew her hands away and swiped her cheeks free of tears. "I don't know why I'm crying," she laughed softly.

"I know why," Jess said. "You finally feel as if your life is beginning again. As if the deepest wish you held inside you is finally real."

Cece sighed as she sat straighter in the chair. "That's precisely how I feel," she acknowledged.

"Our lives are changing," Vin commented as she sat straighter too. "The nest we've built here is growing, and although it's frightening to see my sisters throwing themselves from it like fledglings, it's beautiful too."

"Yes, beautiful," Jess agreed. And she couldn't help remembering the way Cadoc had held her after their interlude last night, and the way she'd felt in his arms. Safe, and blossoming at the same time.

"I know you snuck out last night, sister," Vin said as she turned an eagle-eyed gaze to Jess, as if she was trying to peer into her very soul. "And I think something happened between you and that roguish inventor during the game of hide and seek, yesterday."

Jess reclined and rubbed her hands over her face. "Something did happen, and it's why I snuck away last night. Because it wasn't enough and he promised me another lens. I went to retrieve it."

Cece scanned her face. "What happened when you went to claim it?"

"I came face to face with how foolish and oblivious I've been. With the fact that this wager has rearranged and cauterized everything I thought I knew about myself and what I wanted."

"Which is?" Vin prompted.

"That the reason I'm so fascinated by dragonflies isn't just about their singular beauty," Jes paused to gather her thoughts and tapped a finger against her chin. "It's also about the way their lives are so brief and their entire existence is about making every moment count."

"That is how this man makes you feel?"

Cece's question was full of calm knowing, and a gentle smile curled her lips.

"Yes," Jess answered with a sigh. "He makes me feel like a fledgling."

"You're both on the verge of claiming the lives you want. Just like Arie and Fran," Vin said with a wistful grin.

"What will you do next?"

Jess didn't know how to answer Cece's question, because she didn't know what awaited her. Not tomorrow, not even in the next hour. There was a tumult inside her every time she thought of him. "I don't know. I only know that when I'm near him it feels like there are dragonflies in my stomach and in my heart, and it's like taking joy in my hands and shaping it and not caring what the consequences of stealing that joy from the world will feel like."

Now it was Cece and Vin who reached for her hands, and Jess took them in her own, drawing strength from their support and the understanding and love she saw in their expressions.

"We'll stand by you, no matter what," Vin reassured her with a squeeze. "Because we want you to feel those things. You deserve them."

Jess's eyes filled with tears again as she squeezed back. "I don't know what he wants. If he wants anything more than what we've shared."

Vin patted her hand. "We all noticed the way he looks at you. Like he'll die if he looks away. Like you're the brightest, most precious thing he's ever seen. I think he wants more - even if he's too scared to admit it."

"Men are like that, you know," Cece said. "Too wrapped up in their fear and longing to tell us how they feel. Until the world gives them no choice and they have to stand tall and be vulnerable."

Jess looked down at her lap. "Do you think he's capable of that? Being vulnerable with me?"

"Yes," Vin said decidedly. "I think he's already there. Have you spoken of what will happen when the wager ends?"

"Not directly, no. But I want more of him every time I see him. Not just his touch and his kisses, but his hidden pain and sadness as well. I want to wrap my arms around him and shelter the boy he was and the terrible things he's borne witness to."

"You're falling in love," Cece said with another gentle smile. It was full of compassion and made Jess's heart hurt anew.

"And I think he's falling in love with you as well," Vin observed. "Take it, Little Sister. Cling to it with both hands and don't let it slip away."

There was something in Vin's eyes Jess had never seen. Something she usually hid behind her mask of bravado.

"I will," Jess said with determination. "I will," she repeated.

# Chapter Twenty

T HE NEXT MORNING, CADOC didn't want to rouse from dreams of her. She'd haunted him all night, and letting go of the promise of holding her through the velvet darkness of all the nights of his life felt like letting go of something he didn't think he had a right to hold or pin down.

Only the strong bitter taste of coffee against his tongue and the knowledge his sister and niece and nephew were returning that day, moved him to rise.

When the children wrapped their arms around his waist, he cherished the clasp of their hands at his sides.

Caris watched him with soft eyes. "What has changed, brother? You are not the same as you were when we left."

He shook his head, silently telling her he'd share his turmoil later. Over whisky before the fireplace in the library. She nodded in response, and leaned forward to kiss his cheek. "It gladdens my heart to see you emerge from the shadows, Cadoc," she whispered.

He stepped back, so she wouldn't see how her words filled him with fragile hope.

"Shall we go to the evening service tonight?"

Caris watched him closely. "The evening service?"

"The vicar and his sister have been ill, and there was no service last week. He's scheduled a sermon today and I'd like to go with you and the children."

Her eyes filled with wonder. "She's the one changing you. Yes, we'll accompany you - I want to see the changes she's wrought for myself."

Cadoc ducked his head and ignored her joyful smile. His dragonfly, because he couldn't stomach the thought of her belonging to anyone but him, had changed him. And he didn't know the depth of the change or who he would become without her by his side. He wanted to lose himself in her. Not just her touch and the way she felt pressed against him, but the way sunset caught the hazel gleam of her eyes and the way she held herself still when she was trying to hold onto her dignity. Not just the gasp of surrender she'd made, sweet and low when she'd found her release against his mouth, but the animation and intelligence written all over her face when she spoke of teaching and her infernal bugs.

The service did not unfold as expected. A flurry the likes of which the parish had never seen enveloped it. The congregation was halfway through the second song when the organist threw her hands in the air and left her bench. She stalked toward the vicar, whispering furiously, her finger arrowed in accusation. It was obvious to all that she didn't agree with the song selection. She was making her distaste and exasperation abundantly evident and Cadoc suspected he wasn't the only one who began to think the disagreement was perhaps about more than the song choice. The vicar's eyes widened and he threw up his hands in an attempt to halt the woman's tirade. His lips were moving, but whatever he was saying was inaudible to the congregation. If he was attempting to pacify her, Cadoc mused, he was failing miserably. The vicar was relatively new to the parish, and it was his first assignment and the organist was a buxom widow with a mind and hearth of her own. There was clearly something unfolding between them.

Cadoc had known the moment Jess and her sisters had slid onto the bench directly behind him, and his entire body had tingled with sharp awareness at her closeness. He decided to take advantage of the chaos and turn around so he could steal a look at her. When he did, she met his gaze, and pushed past her sisters with muttered apologies. They all gave her indulgent looks and shooed her in his direction as he stood and made his way to her.

Once they were a few feet apart, he wasted no time. "Come," he said, and pulled her along behind him when she slipped her hand into his.

He dragged her behind the vestibule wing, and only halted once they were ensconced in the vicar's study and he'd closed the door.

"Why do you have such an affinity for cramped, darkened spaces?" She groused.

"Because nooks and crannies protect us from discovery. But this is neither cramped, nor dark," he said as he lit one of the kerosene lamps and pressed her against the edge of the sturdy desk.

"We are in a church full of people and you just pulled me away for all to see. Could you be any less conspicuous?"

"No one noticed. They're enthralled by the fight between the vicar and the organist. If they did notice, they'll assume we're talking about something that has to do with the school. And you didn't have to take my hand, dragonfly," he told her, his voice full of affection.

"Let me guess," she said as she tapped a finger against his chest. "All you could think about was how much of a distraction their argument was, and how suited it was to your unorthodox intentions."

"There's no need for feigned anger, Jess. This is your chance to win back another lens."

"There's only one more. And then you have to hand over the microscope itself," she smugly informed him.

"You're very confident of your ability to resist my kisses," he said as he looked down at her. "Is that all you want? The chance to win back another lens?"

Her gaze never wavered. "Perhaps I want more."

Her confidence set him even more on edge and he pulled her toward him. "I have a confession," he whispered into her ear.

"Another one?" She said with her sudden breathlessness. "You gave me more than a handful of them last night."

"Are you keeping a record?"

"No. Perhaps I grow weary of hearing them. Perhaps I would rather you put your mouth to better use."

"I've dreamt of you drenching my fingers and flooding my mouth. Dreamt of the taste of you as you fall apart beneath my teeth and tongue. Just as you did last night."

"I have a confession as well," she informed him in a sultry tone.

"I hope it's a naughty one. Let's hear it, dragonfly."

"Only if you tell me why you call me that. Is it because I draw them?"

His breath went still at the question and he didn't know if he could answer it truthfully.

"That's part of it, yes. I'll tell you the rest some other time," he finally confessed.

"I want to know if you think of me when you're alone."

"I think of you all the time, not just when I'm alone."

"What happens when you think of me?"

He took her hand and pressed it over the swell of his erection. "This is what happens," he growled.

"Do you tend it? Or do you just box the imaginary foe in your workshop until it goes away?"

"What do you know about tending it?"

He watched her cheeks flame, but she didn't back down. "Doesn't it cause you pain if you don't take care of it?"

He chuckled darkly. "How do you know about blue balls and their effect, dragonfly?"

"Is that what you call them? Do they actually turn blue?"

"Mine have never done so, and I hope they never do. I take myself in hand when attention is required. Now. Enough questions."

She gave him an arch look, but slid her hand behind his neck. "Now that my curiosity has been satisfied on so many levels, resisting you should be easier than slicing pie."

"I don't think I'm the only one who's overconfident in my abilities," he murmured.

"I'll never fathom why you believe yourself so irresistible," she murmured back.

"I don't think I'm irresistible," he confessed. "At least not to everyone. But I am to you, just as you are to me. Because we both feel this thing between us."

"This thing?" She asked with a mischievous smile and dropped her other hand to his waist. "This thing?" She repeated, and stroked the length of him behind his trousers.

He bucked against her touch, all of his senses suddenly alive. "You're playing with fire, dragonfly," he warned.

"Not if I'm the only one who holds the matches, miner," she said as she dropped to her knees in front of him.

Her eyes shone and she licked her bottom lip as she stared at the way he was reacting to her presence. She slid a single finger along his waistband. "There were other illustrations in the books Arie showed us."

"Other illustrations?" He asked, his voice strangled and hoarse.

"Yes," she said with a purr. "Other illustrations. Illustrations of things I've thought about doing to you. Illustrations of things I think will make you beg for your relief against my tongue and my mercy."

Cadoc closed his eyes. If she was proposing what he thought she was proposing, he didn't trust himself to hold onto even the barest vestige of control. He looked down at her, and his breath caught in his chest. Her eyes were more green than gold, and her lips were the dusty pink of the sunset and all he could think about with every atom of his being was what her face would look like when she took his cock in her mouth. "Do it, dragonfly," he entreated. "Make me beg."

She stroked his length through the fabric again, her eyes a trifle hazy on his. "I don't know if I should. I don't think you'll be able to remain silent. There'll be no shouting or groaning. We wouldn't want to arouse more suspicion than we already have."

Her teasing would be the death of him. He held her gaze as he unbuttoned the placket of his trousers and shoved them to his hips. His arousal rose strong and proud between them and he watched as she licked her lips again. He barely stifled his groan.

"Show me how you want to be touched," she commanded.

His hips bucked toward her of their own accord as all the dreams he'd kept buried from the night before flooded him. Cadoc set his hand to his cock and gave it a tight, firm stroke from root to tip. Her eyes glazed even further and she sighed.

"Just like that," she said.

He stroked it again and she leaned forward so he rested against her mouth. When her tongue emerged from her parted lips and she licked around the head of his cock, he surged again and groaned.

"I said you have to be quiet," she remonstrated as those dusty pink lips wrapped around him.

He lifted a fist to his own mouth and bit down on his knuckles as he tangled his other hand in her hair to hold her fast to him.

"Mmmm," she throatily exhaled, and he felt the vibration of her approval all along the length of his throbbing shaft.

Cadoc looked down at her again, her mouth full of his cock, and her eyes on his full of wicked intent, and he surrendered to the sweet suction as she drew him against the roof of her mouth. In that moment, Cadoc knew he was lost and there was no turning back. The knowledge of how wholly he was hers was like an inescapable anvil that weighed him down as he thrust into the warm cavern she offered him.

"I think it is I who will emerge the victor, this time," she said as she leaned away before she took him again.

# *Chapter Twenty-One*

J ESS CLOSED HER EYES and stroked the flat of her tongue against the slick steel of him and knew that she was the one who held all the power. His eyes had closed and his head was tipped back and his fist was in his mouth to stifle the growls he couldn't quite smother. In this, he was wholly hers and she knew she was more than the victor. She was the bloodied conqueror who left ravagement and chaos in her wake.

This was his surrender and her conquest and she relished the sense of triumph. He was truly, irrevocably at her mercy. Just as she had been at his in the library the night before. The sharp knife of joy she suddenly knew was love, slashed through her. Whatever the future held for them, even if it was nothing more than the knowledge he was helpless at her hand, was enough to fill her with a fierce joy she couldn't contain.

His thrusts became more forceful, and she widened her mouth and gripped his cock with her hand before delicately stroking the testes that knocked against her chin with every surge of his hips. He was wild and unhinged and savage and taking from her and falling under her spell at the same time.

"Fuck, dragonfly," he groaned around his fist.

She smiled around his cock because she knew he was completely lost to her. That in this moment he was hers as he had never been anyone's.

Jess kept her gaze on him as his hand slid through her hair. She imagined it was as white-knuckled as the one he held to his mouth and she purred in satisfaction. His face flushed, his eyes squeezed shut and his hand tightened in her upswept curls until she could feel the sting of it, pulling her close as if she were the only thing that would save him from drowning.

"Fuck, dragonfly," he rasped again. "Fucking take me just like that. It's what I dreamt of last night, the sweet slide of my cock down your throat. You on your knees taking me."

His raw confession made liquid pool between her thighs where she knelt on the floor, and Jess angled her jaw to take him more deeply. *Yes, I'll fucking take you,* she confessed silently. *And you'll take me.*

The first drip of his cum was salt and earth and made her think of the dragonflies winging over green summer grass. His hips rocked against her, and he filled her mouth and her heart with the power of his surrender. When he emptied himself and pulled away, he feathered his finger over her still wet mouth, his expression reverent. He pulled her to her feet, and kissed her temple and the side of her jaw. "You ruin me, dragonfly."

Jess wasn't ready to confess he ruined her too, so she simply smiled and met his lips. His tongue stroked into her mouth. "The taste of my cum in your mouth," he growled as his hand fell to her waist and began rucking up her skirt.

"I'm going to return the favor," he promised as his fingers found her wet and open.

He yanked her harder against him. "Taking my cock made you so fucking wet and even more perfect," he said. "Let me make you come too, love."

That rumbled endearment skated over her and Jess wanted nothing more than to be his love. She spread herself wider and let herself fall against the desk as he dropped to his knees.

When his mouth landed on the throb between her legs, it was more than it had been the night before. Seeing him worship her in the light of day, knowing she'd filled his dreams and been the one to unmake him and render him senseless to all but her touch, heightened her arousal.

He lifted her leg to his shoulder and swept his tongue across her clitoris before sucking it into his mouth. Jess lifted her hips against him and fisted her hands in his hair to hold him just where she wanted him.

He chuckled against her. "Yes, dragonfly, show me how you want me to make you lose yourself," he said before he swiped his tongue over her once more.

Jess could feel how close she was, feel the rise of the wings in her chest and stomach as she moaned.

"Now I'm the one who must tell you to be quiet," he admonished with a laugh as he lifted her hand to her mouth and pressed it against her lips.

Jess held her hand to her mouth and let her head fall back on her shoulders.

His grip on her ankle was secure and safe and his mouth was heaven as it slicked over her, hot and sweet and fierce.

"Mine," he growled against her.

*Yes, I'm yours,* she confessed to herself. *I'll only ever be yours.* She was still too afraid to give him the words, but she held them and savored them. Just as she was savoring him and he was savoring her.

He lifted his head and raised his eyes to hers before he slipped two fingers in his mouth. She couldn't look away as he swirled them inside her. His expression was open and he gave her a feral grin before he dropped his head again.

The plunge of his fingers inside her, and the nip of his teeth at her center, was so overwhelming she didn't know if she wanted to push him away or pull him even closer. The pressure built and she gripped him harder, her fingers a tangled vise in the hair at his nape. When her body started quivering beneath his onslaught, and she bit back the sob with her fist, he hummed.

The hum was a caress like the lullaby he'd sung to her the night before, and she broke at its beauty. He swallowed her release, just as he had the night before, his eyes closed in bliss and his face taut with emotion.

When her quaking stopped and she felt wrung out, he scooped her into his arms and carried her to the door. Jess let him back her into it and she closed her eyes as he dipped his thumb into the cleft between her breasts and bit her earlobe.

He dropped his head when she shifted, and groaned against the side of her neck.

His body was flush against hers and the wooden door was rough where it met her elbows. He was hard again, and the bared length of him pressed against her skirts. She wanted to raise them and truly take him into her body.

The incense from snuffed altar candles made of beeswax curled around them, and the harsh abrasion of cedar from the open chest where the vicar stored the vestments tickled her nose. Something tender and breakable filled the air between them, and the hush that fell was full of the threat and promise of words hanging unsaid.

"I will bring you the microscope tomorrow, dragonfly," he said as he pressed a long kiss to her temple before grazing her nose with his own.

Jess wanted to tell him this had grown far beyond her dratted microscope, far beyond their wager. She swallowed the unspoken protest and jerkily nodded her assent.

His lips met hers in a soft kiss and the look in his eyes made her believe he was telling her goodbye. She wanted to howl at the agony and needlessness of it. She wanted to tug him to her again and hear him say she was his. Just one more time. She wanted him to say he was hers. She buried those words too.

He took her hand and opened the door. When he led her back to the sanctuary, it was empty. "Do you think they commented on our absence?"

Cadoc tightened his grasp and reeled her back against him. "Only my sister and yours," he said as he nuzzled the crown of her head.

He turned her about and tipped her chin up. His lips fluttered over the corners of her mouth before they settled against her own. They were firm and she could sense his resolve as he gathered the strength to walk away. If this was to be all they shared, Jess knew she needed to do the same. She broke the kiss and gently scraped her fingers over his shadowed jaw.

"Goodbye, Cadoc," she said as she felt her throat closing up. "I'll see you tomorrow when you deliver my winnings."

She slipped away from him, desperate to escape before the sobs she was biting back fell from her lips. She felt his eyes on her, like an arrow nocked to a bow, on the brink of being loosed, but restrained by an indomitable will.

Jess wrapped her cloak under her chin and nearly ran home. When she got there, she pushed the door closed and leaned against it, finally letting herself feel the emptiness.

She felt bereft and broken and she didn't know if she'd ever feel whole again because of all the wreckage she felt inside her heart.

She let the tears fall silently, her hurt and pain muffled against the wood. She was wiping her eyes when someone gently caressed her arm.

"I know it hurts, dear heart," her sister Cece murmured.

Jess turned and buried her face between her sister's shoulder and neck. "Why does it have to hurt this much?"

"Love always hurts. Until it doesn't. Even then it's still a constant battle," Cece said as she stroked her back.

"I didn't plan on falling in love with him - but I was in the middle of it before I even knew what was happening," Jess raggedly mumbled.

"That's the beauty and the agony of it. It comes upon us when we least expect it and leaves us floundering."

"How am I supposed to live with this? Knowing I'm likely no more than a dalliance to him, and if I'm more than that, he's determined to keep that knowledge to himself and never act on it?"

"Men are obstinate and often ignorant. And as I said yesterday, often truly afraid of surrendering to what they feel."

"I don't know what he feels for me beyond lust. He's said things, but only when he was showing me the strength of his attraction. I don't think I can trust there's more."

"I can't tell you everything will be alright, or assure you that he'll be brave enough to ever tell you how he feels. All I can tell you is that I'm here for you and I'll be here to help you mend yourself if you need to. As will Vin and Emily and Gertie and Arie and Fran."

Jess eased herself from her sister's embrace and wiped away her tears once again. "Thank you."

Cece met her gaze and brushed her hand over Jess's cheek. "You're welcome, dear heart. Find your courage, just as I did with Mal. Let it be your blade."

# *Chapter Twenty-Two*

C ADOC FELT AWKWARD IN her space. He'd packaged her microscope that morning with trembling hands and made himself a resolution to set her free.

She moved through her classroom with brusque efficiency and he wanted to sink through the floor. He set the package he'd brought on the edge of her desk and cleared his throat. "The terms of our wager have been met and I've upheld my end of the bargain."

She whirled around and clasped a hand to her mouth. "You've returned my microscope!"

Her enthusiasm was contagious, and he couldn't hold back his answering grin. "I've polished it for you."

"You needn't have," she said with a furrow between her brows.

"It's the least I could do after my reprehensible behavior."

"I thought we'd established I was a willing participant."

"We have, but I still felt the need to make amends."

She stomped toward him, scowling fiercely. "No amends, Cadoc. Treat me the same way you've been treating me - as an equal."

He stowed his hands in his pockets, so he wouldn't reach out and draw her to him. "You are my equal in everything but experience."

"And we were well on our way to remedying that discrepancy."

She came to a halt in front of him, her breath a thready staccato, her hands twisted in the folds of her skirt.

He couldn't resist touching her. She was too close and too there. He lifted his hand to her cheek and cupped it gently.

"You're impossible to ignore, dragonfly."

She turned her face and kissed his palm. "Will you ever tell me why you call me that?"

"I've already given you that truth."

She shook her head in denial. "Not the whole of it. You promised to tell me all of it when the time was ripe."

"And you think that time is now?"

She shrugged. "It is as ripe as any. If you insist our arrangement is at an end, I want to know why you were so intent on it in the first place."

He stroked his thumb along the curve of her cheek, all the way to her hairline. Her brow was furrowed again, and he wanted more than anything to smooth the crease. He felt the weight of her burdens as keenly as he felt his own, and the urge to lift them from her shoulders undid him. Letting her go would take every ounce of the resolve he'd rebuilt after his family died.

Would telling her how lost he'd become, how irrevocably tied to her he felt, help her? His throat was suddenly dry with the words caught in it, and he became achingly conscious she was waiting for his answer. She deserved it - even if his confession would leave her unsettled and him vulnerable.

"When you talk about them — your whole face lights up and I can see their magic. You're part of that magic too, and you make me feel like the world is full of possibility and enchantment. When you told me about their abbreviated lifespan, you talked about how you admired them for living each day to the fullest. It's what I admire about you too - the way you spread your wings and wrap them around the world. The way you swallow knowledge and radiate compassion. The way you make the space you occupy irrefutably yours."

Her eyes were shining with tears now, and when she arched toward him and kissed the corner of his mouth, he turned his head. "That's truly how you think of me?" She hoarsely whispered against his bottom lip.

"I think you're extraordinary. Let me show you how extraordinary I think you are."

"If I let you, what does that mean?"

"It doesn't have to mean anything," he said. Even as he longed to tell her it would mean everything. That her complete surrender would rearrange his world.

"Then show me. I may never have another chance."

He tipped her chin up so he could study her face. Her expression was resolute.

"I'm locking the door."

Once he'd secured the deadbolt, he stalked toward her.

She stood her ground and released her grip on her skirts. "What about the windows?"

"It's nearly dusk and soon we'll be obscured from view," he assured her as he slid his palm from her shoulder to the button at her throat. She leaned into his touch.

"Will you unbutton me? It's what I wanted that first afternoon - when we made our wager."

He'd been craving the velvet of her skin, and was only too eager to oblige. He ran his forefinger over the closure at her throat. The jet button was secured with a bit of lace he knew her sister Cece had tatted. It was dyed a mottled cream, like weak tea, and set off the wine dark color of her dress.

He loosed it slowly from the lace and slipped his finger along the edge of her corset. Her hand moved over his as she unfastened the second button. He pushed it away and shook his head. "No. You asked me to do it and I'll go at my own pace."

She quirked a brow in challenge, but lowered her hands to her waist again. "I've been patient my whole life and my patience is running out."

He swiftly unmoored the rest of the buttons, thankful for the haste that concealed his trembling.

The sleeves were tight, but he wrestled her arms free, one at a time. When he pushed the shirt from her shoulders, she let it fall to the floor behind her.

Her brows were level, but he could sense she was still challenging him. She untaped her skirt and it joined her shirt. Now it was only her corset, her shift, her crinoline and her petticoat. Still too many layers.

She stepped away and motioned toward him. "What of you?"

He pulled off his overcoat and laid it over the desk behind him. When he set his hands atop the buttons of his waistcoat, she crossed her arms and Cadoc decided to give her the show she was so impatient to receive. His plain cotton shirt was next and once it had joined the rest of his clothes, he bracketed his hips with his fists.

Her gaze went to his bare chest, and he couldn't resist flexing it in response. A wry smile curved her lips as she unlaced her corset.

"You may take care of the rest," she said as she dropped it behind her.

"I thought you'd never ask."

He scraped his knuckles up her sides, and relished the flutter of her pulse and the gooseflesh that rose in the wake of his touch.

Cadoc wanted to map and catalog every inch of her, above the cotton and below it.

"Do you have any affection for this shift?" He asked as he fingered the shapeless collar.

"No, it is the oldest one in my closet and due for replacement."

"Exactly what I hoped you'd say."

He grasped the edges of her collar again and tore it. The fabric was nearly threadbare and ripped easily, baring her to him.

She was smirking. "Now I'll have to fashion something to go beneath my corset."

"We'll make do. I'll steal one of my sister's if I need to - the house is less than a quarter mile from the schoolhouse."

"My dishabille won't require such drastic measures. All of my sisters but Vin are elsewhere, and she is supremely aware of our wager."

"Then I have your permission to dispose of this in a similar fashion?" He tapped her petticoats and crinoline.

She shook her head. "No, these aren't as easily replaced. I'll divest them myself."

He stepped away so he would have the memory of her fingers working efficiently over her remaining undergarments. When she kicked them aside he raised a hand- bading her to let him absorb what she'd revealed.

She clasped her arms over her breasts and imperiously tilted her chin.

Dusk had fallen, and the soft amber light gilded her in shadow. It rippled over her like silk and his breath caught in his throat.

She was arrestingly perfect, a study in contrasts. Her hair was half undone, and snaked over her shoulders and chest - a deep mahogany waterfall. She had a habit of biting her nails, and the pale pink crescents were nearly translucent against her rosy skin. Her eyes were hooded, the hazel gleam hidden beneath the dark sweep of her lashes.

"You are utter perfection, dragonfly. Crafted to drive a man to drink with longing. Or purgatory."

"It's merely a thing of science and natural order," she protested.

"You are not merely anything," he said as he crept closer once more.

When he lifted his hand to the mahogany waterfall that had held him transfixed, it trembled slightly. When he tangled his fingers in one of the wayward strands of her hair, he felt her tremble in response. She bit her lip, and the vivid pink left behind was irresistible.

His mouth landed softly on hers. A quest and a farewell. He knew he needed to make this vision of her enough, that she had won the wager and he was letting her go.

His tongue stroked against hers and when he clasped her hips to draw her closer, her hands fell away. Her breasts were crushed against his chest and he could feel the heat of their tips raking over him. He knew they'd become abraded, and even rosier, where they slid through the mat of dark hair that curled over his torso.

He still wore his trousers and she set her hands to the waistband.

The sudden banging on the door jolted them apart, and as she only just managed to lift her discarded blouse to shield her body when St. Simon came crashing through the door. Cadoc briefly resolved to install a better dead-bolt on the schoolhouse door before turning to face their intruder.

"I knew I couldn't trust you to leave her unscathed," St. Simon thundered as he strode toward them.

His fist landed against Cadoc's temple and Jess gasped.

"No, Thaddeus. It's what I want."

St. Simon turned to her in fury. "It may be what you want, Jess. But he's taken advantage of you and he'll do the right thing. He'll be made to do the right thing," the man muttered as he turned back to Cadoc.

"I don't care what your intentions have been toward my sister-in-law, Morgan. But I'll tell you what they are now. You will wed her. You've ruined her and you'll face the consequences of it."

"You have no right, Thaddeus!" Jess shouted.

But Cad knew Thaddeus had every right. That he was protecting his sister, just as Cad had protected his own. He knew the scene her brother-in-law had interrupted was damning. And that it had been imminent.

He held his hand to his jaw and nodded. "You're right. I knew what I was doing and I couldn't stay away. I'll do the right thing."

St. Simon nodded in agreement. "You will. If I have to drag you kicking and screaming to the altar myself. I'll see you at the cottage in the morning."

He turned back to Jess. "I'll give you the privacy to gather yourself, together Jess. Then you're coming back to the farm with Arie and I."

Jess clenched her fists at her sides. "I'm a grown woman, Thaddeus. This is not your place."

He shook his head and gave her a tender smile even Cad could sense was filled with affection.

"It is my place, Jess. Arie would expect no less."

He turned back to Cad with a glare. "Tomorrow," he snarled as he pointed a finger in his direction.

Cad gulped but nodded in agreement. "Tomorrow," he agreed.

# Chapter Twenty-Three

After Thaddeus had sent Cadoc on his way, he bundled Jess into his waiting carriage. Arie was already there, nestled against the squabs, her new babe in her arms.

"Sit," Arie said, and patted the seat beside her.

"Are you ashamed of me?" Jess asked. She couldn't bear it if that was the truth.

Arie smiled at her just as tenderly as her husband had. "No my little love, I'm not ashamed of you. I could never be ashamed of you. But I refuse to stand by and let you be used by someone who doesn't appreciate you."

Jess brushed her loose hair behind her ears even as her eyes filled with tears at her sister's understanding. "He appreciates me."

Arie raised a brow. "He's finally admitted how he feels then?"

Jess shook her head. "No," she quietly confessed. "I don't know if he feels the same."

"Then Thaddeus and I did the right thing. If he feels the same, he can prove it to all of us tomorrow morning."

"How did you happen to be here?"

"We were retrieving packages in town and Thad didn't like the look of the sky. If you were still at the school, he insisted we would make sure you got home safely."

"You'll have to use lye soap on his eyes. If my brother-in-law had arrived a few moments later he would have an indelible impression of Cadoc's bare arse."

Arie chuckled softly. "I'm happy to see your sense of humor remains intact. You shall have need of it if you end up wed."

Jess leaned back and let the soothing rock of the carriage soothe her to sleep. Just as it was soothing the newest addition to their family. She would decide later what her answer would be when the man she loved, who was too afraid to love her in return, showed up at the cottage as Thaddeus had commanded him to.

⚬

The next morning, she sat before the fire in the cottage kitchen, her hands clasped in her lap for strength. Because she knew she needed to refuse his suit. When she heard his voice echo in the foyer she stared resolutely into the flames of the brazier.

When he dropped to one knee in front of her and took her hand in his, Jess sighed. She still couldn't read the depths of his feelings for her. And she knew her decision was the right one.

"Will you marry me, Jess Wainwright?"

She shook her head. "No, I won't."

"I thought this is what you wanted," he said, his brows drawn together in confusion.

"This is never what I wanted. I only wanted you, freely giving yourself to me. This sham is anything but that."

"Me offering for you, isn't a sham. I'm doing the honorable thing and making everything right. As I'm expected to do."

"I don't want your bloody honor," she scoffed. "It's never been a thing I wanted. I want your honesty and your heart and those are things you're too afraid to pledge."

"You heard her," St. Simon said from the doorway.

Cadoc, turned, still down on one knee and glared at him. "You're the one who was so adamant about this."

"Because I wanted her to have options. As every woman should. If she's said this gesture isn't enough, then it isn't. And it's her choice to make."

Cad rose to his feet. It was obvious he wanted to return the punch Thaddeus had delivered, and was barely restraining himself from lashing out. "Then her ruination, the one you were so desperate to prevent, is on your head."

In that moment, Jess resolved that she would have him wholly. At least the part of him that was hunger and desire.

———◆———

After Thaddeus and Arie returned her to the cottage, she snuck into the night. "Why are you here? I gave it back. Every single piece. And what have I told you about wandering about in the cold and the dark?"

His tone was bitter and he was practically snarling. But why would he care whether she traipsed into the night alone? *Unless he cared.*

He hadn't bothered to button his shirt, and for a moment Jess was transfixed by the play of starlight over the expanse of muscle. He was gripping the neck of a bottle of whisky.

"I'm not here about the microscope."

"Then why are you here, dragonfly?"

His expression was inscrutable, his eyes red-rimmed and he smelled like he'd been swimming in a barrel of liquor instead of drinking it.

"Because this thing between us is unresolved."

"You turned me down. Loudly and publicly in front of your sister and her family."

"Because you offered to marry me out of a sense of responsibility." She stepped closer. "But that doesn't mean I don't want other things."

He closed his eyes and the deep breath he took made the shirt flutter. When he opened them, they were brimming with despair and resignation. "What if I don't want to give you those things? What if I don't want to hurt you any more than I already have?"

Jess closed the door and pushed past him. "I accepted the wager. You may have pressured me into it, but it was something I wanted. Even if I couldn't admit it to myself." This time when she drew near, he flinched.

"I manipulated you, Jess. You didn't have a choice because I didn't give you one. I have to live with that. From the very beginning I knew you would be the victim of its end. I knew the shame and the tragedy would all be heaped on your shoulders.And I still let my selfishness jeopardize everything you've worked for. I know I was wrong and I can't forgive myself for the damage I caused."

She braced her hands on her hips and tipped her chin toward him at a mutinous angle. "I am an independent woman and willing to take responsibility for my own actions. Every decision I made was a step I eagerly took. You didn't coerce me."

The supple curve of his mouth thinned into a brittle line. "It was coercion, Jess. I forced your hand just as I've been battering my way into places denied me my entire life. I've never cared to examine the consequences of my actions. Until now when they've barred me from the one thing I want the most."

Jess placed her hand in the middle of his chest and felt the warm flex of muscle beneath it. She'd expected his flesh to be cool to the touch, like marble, because of the starlight. It wasn't. It was as warm and golden as she remembered.

She slid her fingers to his waistband and his jaw tightened. She curled her fingers around the edge of his trousers and he tipped his head back and clenched the hand not holding the bottle. She tapped her fingernails against the warm, golden skin, because she couldn't resist touching him, and he quivered, like a taut bowstring. When she pushed, he stepped backward, as if he couldn't resist her either.

"It wasn't coercion, Cad. I wanted you then, and I want you now. To hell with my reticence and everything and everyone telling me you're unworthy of my affection. *Or that I shouldn't want this.*"

He groaned, and the bottle slipped from his hand. It shattered on the floor and the liquid splashed and sloshed all over her skirt. He didn't give her time to protest or exclaim. His hands rose to her face and bracketed it before he swooped. His lips captured hers and he groaned again.

He spun her away from the door, kicked it closed and then swung her back around to pin her against it.

He groaned again, mumbled something monosyllabic and incoherent into the kiss, and the solid weight of his palm slid over her thigh. She felt it through the layers of her clothing, like a brand so hot the flames were the eerie white color fierce enough to shape metal.

When he curled her leg around his waist, she clung. She longed to feel him there, just there, more than she needed her next breath. The stars swirling through her brain were an echo of the sky she'd walked under to be with him tonight, and all of the desire she'd kept banked coalesced into a single, luminous point of light.

"I am bad for you, Jess Wainwright. This will only hurt you more, ruin you and your chances."

She tipped away from the kiss and snaked her fingers around his stubborn, cleft chin. "I choose this, Cadoc Morgan. Just as I've been choosing it all along. I'll choose my own chances and determine my own ruin."

"I'll not ask again. I've imagined you for too long, and we're not in a closet or a crowded church or your school-room, wary of discovery."

"I want you to show me all the things you've been dreaming about. And more of the things you keep whispering about and tempting me with."

She took one of his empty hands in hers and raised it to her lips. She feathered kisses over his scarred knuckles and mangled fingers and he closed his eyes again at the bliss of her touch.

"And I brought this," she said.

When he opened his eyes again, she was pulling a sheath from her pocket.

"Why? When you've already refused me."

"Because I know this is all you can give me right now. So I'm taking it."

His lips crashed against hers again and he lifted her into his arms. She pressed light kisses against his jaw and his throat as he carried her up the stairs. He nearly stumbled as he thudded against the banister and she giggled.

When he swallowed her laughter with another kiss, the effervescent joy of it nearly shattered her. "Hush, before we wake the house, dragonfly," he admonished as he closed the door of his bedroom behind them.

"Make me hush, Cadoc," she teased.

"I plan on it. Until you're writhing with it," he promised.

He set her on her feet and twirled her around so he could attack the row of buttons at her back. She leaned her neck against his shoulder and pressed back against his already torrid length.

"Dragonfly," he warned. "I want to make this last."

She laughed as he slipped the last button from its hole and let her blouse fall to the floor before she scampered out of reach. "My turn," Jess said.

She could see him holding himself still, like a looming predator and the rigid line of his jaw nearly broke her with want as she pushed his shirt from his shoulders. When she pressed her lips to his chest, and sank to the floor as she followed the trail of dark hair that disappeared into his breeches, he groaned.

She unfastened his trousers next, and after she tugged them to his hips, she palmed his erection.

He watched, captivated and enthralled, as she lifted the sheath and rolled it over him. The way she then pulled it snug and tied it at his base with a sultry smile was all it took for him to throw her onto the bed when she rose to her feet.

Her limbs went akimbo and her feet tangled in her skirts as she fell laughing onto his rumpled satin sheets.

He fell on her before rolling her to the side so he could untape her as swiftly as possible. She made it nearly impossible for him to finish, throwing her head back to nip at his jaw and thrusting her luscious arse against his cockstand. When he'd shed her of her skirt and crinoline, he set his hands to her front, teasing her breasts as he unlaced them where they played peekaboo against her corset.

"Take off your shift and pantlets if you don't want them torn to shreds," he growled in her ear as he stroked her nipples where they chafed against the nearly thread-bare cotton.

She shimmied to her knees and lifted the shift over her head, and then stretched her legs toward him with a teasing smile. "You can remove these. But no ripping things to shreds."

Jess knew he wanted to disobey, to fall on her like a ravening beast, and she licked her lips as she watched him weighing the advantages of rebellion. With a great sigh, he carefully began rolling them down her legs. She knew the only reason he was succumbing to her wishes was because he knew if he destroyed them she wouldn't allow him to replace them.  As soon as he tugged them over her feet he wrapped his hands around her ankles and pulled her toward him, looping her legs around his waist so she was straddling him.

Her heat brushed against him and she wondered fleetingly if he wished she'd said yes, so he could feel the tight clench of her bare skin as she seated his cock deep inside her. She wondered if this was to be his one and only night with her, if he'd accept her gift, and if the memories would be enough to keep her warm every night of her life.

"Put me inside you," he demanded.

"Shouldn't you make me ready first?"

He didn't answer, he just set his hands to her hips and pulled her up the length of his body, until her dripping cunt was right there at this mouth. The word felt naughty in her head, but nothing else sounded appropriate for how fiercely she wanted this. How fiercely she was going to take it.

"Hang onto the headboard, dragonfly," he growled.

He watched as she stretched her arms out and grabbed the cast iron. When he was satisfied her grip was secure, he tightened his hold on her hips to keep her steady and licked through her folds strong and sure.

Jess couldn't muffle her moan of relief as she ground herself against the suction of his lips and tongue. He settled his mouth over the hood of her clitoris and tucked it against the back of his teeth before he bit down ever so gently. "Come for me, dragonfly," he growled. "Make my path smooth and slick and easy."

Her body responded to the savage stroke of his tongue before she was ready, flooding his mouth as he swallowed her release. He gave her clitoris one final lick before he began to ease from beneath her body. She began to move too, but he set his hands on her hips again. "No. Stay just as you are."

This time it was her turn to obey and she did, even though this too was like none of the illustrations she'd seen.

He rose behind her and pushed her legs further apart. When she looked over her shoulder, her gaze met his and their reflection in the mirror hanging on the wall at his back. He gave her a wicked grin.

"That's it, dragonfly. Watch your body take me."

He dipped a finger inside her first, hitting a spot that made her writhe against his hand the way she'd writhed against his face.

"Christ, you're beautiful," he rasped as he slid in another finger. Jess kept her gaze on their reflection so she could see the way his whole body was tense with muscle behind her, his face flushed, his expression intense and his eyes hooded. She felt like a nymph being readied for a rutting satyr - like the ones in her sister Gert's mythology books.

"Are you ready? I can't hold on much longer."

She nodded, because the rough cadence of his voice rendered her mute.

He set one hand on her hip and fisted the other in her loose hair. "Ride me, little dragonfly."

He entered her in one long glide, and she felt the small sting of him leaving her hymen behind for all eternity. And then he was fully seated and she felt full and not full enough. She gritted her teeth against the pressure and tossed her head. He lifted his hand from her hip to stroke it down her back, as if she were a skittish mare.

Jess laughed at the thought and wondered for the first time that night who was taming who. Her lover had likely only given her the illusion she was in control. He tugged her back, so her head was nearly resting against his chest, and her body was arched at an almost painful angle. This time when he thrust into her, the hit was deeper and the base of his cock brushed against her clitoris.

"You were playing games," she wailed.

"Hush, sweeting," he murmured and untangled his hand from her hair. "Bite my hand if you need to, but know this. Nothing about this thing between us has ever been a game. Even when I tried to convince myself otherwise and pretended that's all it was."

Jess dug her teeth into the side of his palm and he hissed as he thrust into her again. This time she reared back against him. His fingers dug into her hips and she knew the imprint would linger. Another reminder that this was her last chance to convince him he was made for her.

"I'm coming, dragonfly," he groaned as he dropped his head to the curve of her shoulder. He set his teeth against her nape and the weight of him shuddered over her back before he went still.

"I'm sorry if I hurt you," he mumbled into her shoulder before pressing a kiss there. "I'm sorry you didn't find your release," he said as he drew away from her.

She flipped over as he leaned back and watched him untie the sheath. He tied it tightly and set it aside, his solemn gaze lingering on her face.

"There will be no apologies between us. Not for this," she told him.

He just gave her a wry smile and rose to his feet. "I'll make it up to you," he said over his shoulder as he strode to the washstand.

She leaned her face into her hand and unabashedly watched the flex of his bare ass as he walked away. There was muscle at his hip that rippled every time he took a step and she was fascinated.

He disappeared into the garderobe, and when he emerged, he caught her staring. He came to a stop and braced his hands on his hips. "Should I turn around for you?"

She propped her chin in both hands. "Please."

He spun around several times.

"That's enough for now. I don't want you falling over and breaking something I may need later."

The rich sound of his laughter filled the room before he pounced as he'd threatened to do.

# *Chapter Twenty-Four*

J ESS HADN'T NOTICED MUCH about his bedroom when he'd hauled her, clinging, across its threshold. But now that she was lying on top of him, her chin propped in her hands, she noticed everything. The decadent satin of the sheets against her bare feet. The scar on his chin that gleamed in the smudgy light of the kerosene lantern. The half-smile that hadn't left his face and the way his thumb likely stroked her ribcage.

And the book on the floor. She'd almost stumbled over it - just before he'd caught her and tossed her down. It was the same one on pest control and agriculture she'd returned last week. It was flipped open to the title page and there was a scrap of folded paper inside it. She pushed herself to the edge of the bed and picked it up.

She heard his intake of breath when she started unfolding it.

It was an incredibly accurate, exquisite pen and ink rendering of a Gold-Tipped Garner.

She held it up to his face. "What is this?"

A blush spread across his cheekbones. "The color reminded me of your eyes."

"You drew this? It's much better than my attempts." She turned it so she could study it more closely. "The legs always look like spindles when I draw them, but this is brilliant."

She felt his shrug beneath her and set her hand to his cheek. "Don't pretend this away, Cadoc."

"I'm not," he said. His thumb started stroking a different pattern against her ribcage. "It gave me something to take joy in besides blueprints."

"You could illustrate my article," she tentatively proposed.

"That would mean our association isn't at an end. It would require close collaboration."

"What makes you think I want to be rid of you?"

"How we've been tonight, it doesn't change anything, dragonfly. I'm still a bad bargain. Even worse than the wager we made."

She swirled her fingers through the taper of hair beneath his navel. "I don't think you're a bad bargain, Cadoc."

He tensed beneath her touch. "Then why did you reject my proposal of marriage?"

"I rejected it because I won't be tied to someone who's only making an offer out of a sense of obligation and a means of assuaging their guilt."

Before she could draw another breath, he'd flipped them over and was leaning over her. "That's not why I proposed."

She pushed futilely against the wall of his chest in an attempt to displace him. "Don't lie to me. I saw the look on your face when you realized we'd been caught. You were terrified."

He pushed her arms over her head and held her wrists in place. "I wasn't terrified, Jess. I was elated. I didn't know how I was going to convince you to stay with me once our bargain ended. Your brother-in-law's interruption solved my dilemma." He took a deep breath and cupped her face. "But it changes nothing. Because I'm not what you deserve."

"How can you say that?" She brokenly asked. "Shouldn't I be the one to decide who and what I deserve?"

"If I hadn't cajoled and pressured you into thinking I was the man you deserved, then yes. But I'm not, dragonfly. You deserve so much more than a man who buries himself in his work and bloodies his knuckles against a sack of grain to chase away his demons."

"You are much more than you think you are, miner. I thought I'd shown you that."

"No one is capable of showing me that, Jess," he tenderly pushed a lock of loose hair behind her ear. "No one but myself. And I don't know if I'll ever be able to accept my own forgiveness. I've always forged my own path, and it's been one of survival, not reckoning."

Her body went from pliant to unyielding beneath him. "I won't beg. I'm not a woman made for begging. You'll come to me of your own free will when you realize what you're throwing away."

"You were right to refuse, me dragonfly," he repeated. "And I'll not let you regret your decision or let it haunt you. I deserve to be the one who's haunted."

She pushed against his chest. "Then that's all you'll ever be. A man who's haunted by possibilities because he's too cowardly to want the reality of them. I'll not wait for you," she warned fiercely as she rolled from the circle of his arms.

⫸◆⫷

He let her go because he could do nothing else. Because the long dark night of his soul and the bottles of whisky had shown him he wasn't enough for her. That he was too broken to be enough.

After he'd helped her back into her clothes and released her into George's keeping for safe transport home, he took up the bottle of whisky again.

This morning, he'd left his bed as tumbled and dodgy as he'd felt, and now he was glad of it. He had the memory of her, lying there, laughing and rosy on bedclothes he'd thrashed against and stroked himself to while dreaming of her. It was the perfect elegy and he held onto it as he nursed the whisky. He didn't know if he'd ever be able to sleep in his bed again.

He stared into the cold embers of the dying hearth, steadily swallowing his third bottle of whisky. It was where Caris found him.

"Brother, you're an idiot," she said.

He blinked awake. Bleary from falling asleep on the sofa that wasn't quite long enough and the vestiges of the liquor. "I'll not destroy her."

"Letting her go is destroying her. And you. Can't you see that?" She asked as she took a seat beside him on the sofa and lifted the half-empty bottle from his hand.

"I see no such thing," he stubbornly said.

His sister groaned in exasperation. "Just as I said. Idiotic. Do you think this is what Mam or Griffin would have wanted for you? Surrendering yourself to your family and your work and leaving no room for anything else?"

"It's not about what they would have wanted."

Caris's hand stroked over the broken skin of his knuckles. "Yes, it is. You're so blinded by your sense of duty you can't see how it's rending you apart from the inside out."

Cadoc rested his head against the sofa. "I sang to her. Right here on this sofa. I held her in my arms and I sang to her."

"And you turned her away? A woman who made you sing? I thought better of you, Cadoc."

He knew if he opened his eyes, her expression would be stern.

"You know what I am, Caris," he said with a sigh. "You know what I'm made of."

"Yes, I do, brother. You're made of never giving up on the things you want. Of fighting for them until there's not a shred of fight left in you. You're made of all the dreams Mam and Griffin had for you, and all the years you've shown all of us the way you love us. We love you just as much, Cadoc, but you need to let her love you too."

Cadoc let Caris's words settle inside him. He knew he needed to be brave enough to face the way Jess Wainwright wanted him to belong to her. Brave enough to make the most of every day, just like his dragonfly.

# Chapter Twenty-Five

J ESS BURIED HERSELF IN her work. In her teaching and her studies. She was up until nearly dawn every morning, sketching and writing. She was nearly finished with her article, and as she looked at the pile of drawings at her elbow, the bright memory of the piece of folded paper she'd found, when she thought he was finally hers, burned in her chest.

She knew her sisters worried about the lavender circles beneath her eyes and the way her laughter faltered and died when they tried to raise her spirits. Jess knew she would be fine again. Someday. She had other things to occupy her mind against the intrusion of a gaze like the wounded blue of the sky before a winter storm. Other things to occupy her hands instead of the way the stubble of his jaw felt beneath her touch. She pushed the papers aside and rose to her feet, just as there was a gentle but determined knock at the door.

"Jess, you have a visitor," Vin said through the door.

She tidied herself in the mirror, and braced herself to face the parents of one of her students. Because she knew the one visitor she wanted would never cross her threshold again. "Coming," she called.

When she walked into the parlor. It wasn't one of her students. Or their parents. It was him.

He turned to face her and he looked as bereaved and stricken with grief by things lost as she felt. His eyes, that wounded blue she couldn't forget, roamed over her in disbelief and awe.

"You haven't changed."

"I have changed," she corrected as she took the seat he gestured toward.

She perched on the edge of the chair, too afraid to lean forward, too afraid to tell him more.

He walked forward and dropped to his knees. When he laid his head in her lap, and sighed like it was the only place in the world he wanted to be, she clenched her fists in her skirts. Just as she'd done that fateful day in her classroom.

"Why are you here?" She asked around the knot in her throat.

He lifted his head and his eyes were red-rimmed. That's when she knew sleep had escaped him too. That the dreams never left him alone, just as they crowded her.

"I'm here because I've been an idiot. Just like my sister said. Just as your sister told me a few moments ago. I finally apologized to your murderous sister Lavinia, and I don't think she's going to poison me." His mouth quirked in a half smile and his chest expanded in a deep breath.

Jess barely dared hope he was finally going to be brave.

"You are an idiot," she agreed. "But I thought we'd already established that."

"I'm an idiot because I can't stay away. Because staying away from you is making me die slowly inside. I'll take anything, dragonfly. Even if it's only your friendship. But I want more than that because you're so much more," he mumbled against her knee. "You're everything."

"I'm everything?" Jess wasn't going to let him off so easily.

He raised his head again and clasped her knee through her skirts. "Everything, dragonfly," he repeated and pulled a rolled sheaf of papers from the pocket of his overcoat.

She took the sheaf and unfurled it. When she did, the tears closed up her throat again. "What is this?" Jess hoarsely asked.

"Your dragonflies. I tore apart my library looking for references. And when I'd exhausted it, I wrote to every scientific society I could think of, asking for more. I drew every single one of them."

"Why would you do that?" She asked as her eyes met his.

"Because I want to be part of you and this," he gestured toward the papers she was clutching. "Because I want to be the man that strives to be enough for you and gives you the strength to become all the things I know you can become."

"You want to be all of those things, but you still haven't said the words I want to hear," she confessed in a strangled breath.

He grasped her knee again. "I love you, dragonfly. I love you so much it hurts when I breathe. I love you so much I can't think of anything but you and nothing I do banishes the thought of you. I'm begging you to let me prove how much I love you."

"How will you do that? What if I don't think this groveling is enough?" Jess sharply asked through her almost tears.

He tipped his head back and closed his eyes. When he opened them again he laughed harshly. "Then I'll grovel and grovel until it is. Until you finally tell me it's enough and you're giving me another chance. I want to help you catalog every species of dragonfly there is. I want to take you fishing and watch the sunlight in your hair, and make you laugh."

She leaned forward and cupped his stubbled jaw and stared directly into his red-rimmed eyes. "You're enough, Cadoc. You've always been enough."

"Thank Christ," he mumbled as he rose to his feet and gathered her in his arms.

She nestled there, in the crook between his shoulder and his neck, as her heart thudded to the rhythm of his. She laid her hand over that reverberation, to reassure herself that he was truly there and finally, irrevocably hers. "I don't want to wait for the banns."

He hummed in laughter, not harsh this time, but relieved. "I'll call in every favor I have to procure a special license," he promised as he kissed the crown of her head.

When Jess lifted her head, his lips met hers. His kiss had the same softness that had fluttered against hers when she left him at the church, when he'd kissed her farewell for the final time two weeks ago. But this wasn't a kiss of farewell, it was one of bravery.

# Notes to Reader

ONE OF THE MOST frequent questions I receive from readers is, "Why don't you write about dukes and the ton?"

Without diving into a quagmire, I'll try to give you a succinct answer: I don't write about dukes and the ton because I find it hard to relate to them. I'm from a working class family and ninety-nine percent of my forebears were either farmers or tradesmen. I want to explore stories about what their lives were like and the ways they were similar to my own.

Now on to a brief summary of the extensive research that went into the backdrop and characters of this book.

I. Jess's profession as a teacher and mandatory public schools in England.

Jess's profession wasn't formalized until the official passage of the Public Schools Act in 1868. Prior to the passage of that act, most village schools originated from the belief of the clergy that every man, woman and child should be literate enough to read the bible. Village schools began as Sunday schools, and by 1839, Parliament was providing annual funding for their continuation. In 1862, the government sought to enforce more oversight in the administration of these semi-parochial schools and introduced standardized testing. By the end of the sixth standard, boys and girls who attended the school were expected to be able to read, write, and calculate basic arithmetic. The girls were also expected to be competent at needlework.

In Chapter One, Jess points out to Cadoc that many of her students have gone on to a secondary education. Most of those students would have attended what was known as a "training school", and some may have apprenticed under Jess or another teacher before being accepted. Training schools gave individuals with a working class background the opportunity to earn a teaching certificate.

II. Child labor in the Welsh mines.

The compact size and stature of children meant they were ideally suited to work in the more cramped spaces of a mine. This included the narrow shafts that went from the pit to the surface. Because enlarging these shafts meant extra expenditures the mine owners would rather apply toward the expansion of the mine itself, they weren't suited for adults to stand in or navigate.

I went down a rabbit hole on Hoopla and checked out *From the Cradle to the Coalmine: The Story of Children in Welsh Mines* by Ceri Thompson. Children as young as five operated the ventilation gates and were often crushed by the heavy carts being hauled through them. The mining shafts were so narrow and steep, the coal was hauled up by boys with a harness attached. The average age of these boys was about twelve years old.

Because of pressure in Parliament from wealthy mine owners, mining wasn't included in the child labor reform law, the 1833 Factory Act. In 1840, Lord Ashley finally convinced Parliament to set up a Royal Commission to investigate the working conditions of children employed in the mining industry. The resulting report was the first government report to include pictures, and was finally published in 1842, in spite of attempts to repress it.

The law was finally passed in 1842 and banned all females and boys under ten from working underground, established a Commissioner of Mines whose duty was to conduct regular inspections, and prohibited anyone under the age of fifteen from being in charge of machinery.

III. Eisteddfod and englyn

The first eisteddfod happened in 1176 when Rhys ap Gruffydd invited singers and poets to his castle in Cardigan for a feast and a competition. The eisteddfod that Cadoc and his family would have been familiar with evolved around 1789.

Today, the National Eisteddfod is one of the largest cultural celebrations in the world, and can draw upwards of ten thousand contestants.

The englyn is a traditional Welsh form of short poetry that uses quantitative meters and certain rhyming patterns that must be adhered to. The englyn penfyr that Cadoc's brother composed for the competition is always a stanza of three lines. The first line consists of ten syllables, traditionally in two groups of five, the second line has between five and six syllables, and the third line has seven syllables. Syllables seven through nine of the first line introduce the rhyme that is repeated on the last syllable of the other two lines.

IV. Victorian methods of contraception

Contrary to popular belief, the coitus interruptus method, or "pulling out", wasn't the only means of contraception. There were several treatises on the subject written in the first third of the nineteenth century. The first such treatise was a series of pamphlets and handbills published and distributed by Francis Place in 1823, and highlighted the benefits of using a sponge for the British working class. By this time, the well-travelled upper classes were well acquainted with the use of a sponge. A small segment of sponge was attached to a ribbon and soaked in a spermicidal mixture such as alum and water. The detriment the use of alum caused to women who used this mixture wasn't identified until decades later.

By far the most popular of these guides to contraception was Richard Carlisle's *Every Woman's Book*. It sold over ten thousand copies and recommended condoms, coitus interruptus and the sponge method.

In 1834, Charles Knowlton's *Fruits of Philosophy* introduced the use of the vaginal douche. It was nothing more than a syringe that squirted a spermicidal mixture shortly after intercourse. (The recommended time was between five and ten minutes immediately after the act.) The solutions recommended for the syringe were alum and water, sulphate of zinc with water, vinegar and water, sodium bicarbonate (saleratus) with water, or liquid chloride with water. The woman squatted over a bowl to perform the ablution.

The first mention of a condom is in reference to King Minos of Crete. Contemporary texts of the time tell us that his wife Pasiphae used a goat's bladder because his semen was said to contain '"scorpions and serpents." Egyptians dyed glans caps in a variety of colors to distinguish amongst the classes and to protect themselves from bilharzia, or parasitic worm infestations. During the English Civil War there was an outbreak of syphilis among soldiers. To combat the outbreak, condoms made of fish, cattle and sheep intestine were distributed to soldiers.

Condoms have been called wetsuits, jimmies, rubbers, nightcaps and all kinds of other things. But the name "condom" comes from an actual historical figure. King

Charles II of England became so conflicted by the number of his illegitimate offspring, he sought out the physician, Colonel Condom. Colonel Condom knew the sheathes made of animal material had been used to prevent venereal disease, and prescribed them to the monarch for contraceptive use as well.

Condoms began to be sold wholesale in the late eighteenth-century, and a female merchant, Mrs. Phillips, became the most prominent supplier when she opened a warehouse on the Strand. These early condoms were almost exclusively formed from animal intestines.

When Charles Goodyear invented rubber vulcanization, the use of intestines began to fall out of favor. Vulcanization consists of heating together sulfur and natural rubber to create a more malleable and durable material. By 1860, condoms were being produced on a large scale, and were popular because they were cheaper than condoms made from intestines or bladder and could be reused. Skin condoms became outdated by the end of the nineteenth-century.

I will discuss the widespread use of abortifacients used in one of my Substack posts. These are delivered to your mailbox as a newsletter if you're not on the app, so make sure you're subscribed to my newsletter if you want more details. You can subscribe via the drop down menu in the upper left hand corner of my website.

V. Women and Entomology

Jess's catalog of dragonflies was inspired by the historical figure, Eleanor Ormerod.

Eleanor's first scientific publication was a treatise on the poisonous secretions of the Triton newt. She tested her hypotheses on both her cat and herself, and even put the tail of a live newt into her mouth. The effects of that tail, which included foaming at the mouth, oral convulsions and an aching head, were all carefully described in the paper.

The many insect collecting walks Eleanor went on meant she frequently interacted with the farming community. Farmers often complained to her about their pest problems and she realized they were in need of science-based advice for protecting their crops. Eleanor decided to practically apply what she'd learned from her observations and own 1877 she began publishing a series of annual reports with methods of agricultural pest control recommended and explained.

Eleanor based her recommendations on questionnaires she circulated in agricultural communities all over the country that asked farmers to document the pests they had observed and how they'd attempted to manage them. She took this crowdsourced ground-level data and meshed it with her own knowledge to offer practical advice. Her recommendation for the use exclusion nets and manual removal formed the backbone of modern, environmentally friendly, integrated pest management strategies.

# *Acknowledgements*

Every single book is inspired by my own love story. A single mom working her tail off who met someone who said "I'll be there no matter what." Anthony, you make my life better and richer and more wonderful than I ever could have imagined. These last twenty-seven years we have been through things we didn't anticipate and couldn't have predicted, but your love has both kept me grounded and given me wings.

Thank you from the bottom of my heart to my amazing ARC Team — you drop everything when one of my books lands in your email. I don't ask for it, and I don't expect it, and I am eternally grateful for your support and kindness.

# *Meet the author*

Andrea loves writing sassy, independent women and complex, layered heroes who guard their hearts. She loves diving into obscure research and telling stories that readers don't expect to find.

She loves hearing from readers! You can email her at authorandreajenelle@gmail.com

You can find her books in your library via Hoopla and Libby and on all digital book platforms.

# Other Books by Andrea

<u>Willow Creek Series (in order, but can be read in any order as standalones)</u>

No Regrets

No Surrender

No Promises

No Shadows

No Doubts

No Excuses

No Angels (Christmas novella in Kindle Unlimited)

Twelve Days & Twelve Nights (Christmas novella in the Wreck My Halls anthology)

No Apologies (releasing June 2025)

No Ghosts (Halloween novella releasing in the One Dark Night anthology Sept. 2025)

No Dreams (releasing October 2026)

No Strings (releasing June 2027)

<u>The Wainwright Sisters (Victorian era historical romance)</u>
When Araminta Greaves Traded Her Dignity for Bliss
How Frances Wainwright Learned to Love
Cece Wainwright's Christmas Wish
When Jess Wainwright's Curiosity was Satisfied (releasingFeb. 2025)
How Gert Wainwright Spent Her Holiday (releasing November2025)
When Lavinia Wainwright Went Missing (releasing June 2026)
Emily Wainwright's Exemplary Education (releasing November2026)
<u>Sons & Daughters of Lir (paranormal urban romantasyinspired by Celtic mythology)</u>
Way Down We Go
Wither on the Vine
The Berserker's Daughter (prequel novella releasing August2025)
Untitled Book 3 (releasing 2026)
Untitled Book 4 (releasing 2027)
<u>The Terrible Trentons</u>
Spine of Steel (releasing April 8 on Kindle Unlimited-Book one in the Suffragette Uprising Series)
Since the Day You Left (novella included in the Ordered Home for Christmas anthology – releasing October 2025)

www.ingramcontent.com/pod-product-compliance
Lightning Source LLC
Chambersburg PA
CBHW060304310726
48976CB00007B/2204